The Lightning Eater

Vol. 2

The Edge of Sanctuary

Forward From the Author

The stories of Sunlatveria and the family that dwell about are a result of years of writing and research collected across a field of different studies and interests. I know little of the heritage behind my last name. The stories of Sunlatveria manifested years before the first book came about. My passion for writing came about around age ten after a school teacher read in class several full-length books over the course of weeks. By age twelve I'd created a paradise of power and unlimited imagination that could rival the ancients while dominating the future all at the same time.

High school and a year at Columbia only moved this forward as teachers pushed me to read and write more as I attended a variety of literature centric classes. Many names within the books are taken from friends and loved ones alike. In the end this series is a tribute to all the stories, characters and settings that moved and comforted me as a child.

Book two is owed to the most beloved. To Clementine, I realized upon first seeing you that I had truly never felt love, only lust, obligation and comradery. For years I've wanders in fog, unsure of everything, you provide me with a light unlike any other. When you read this, know that I love you, I'll always love you and no matter what, my life will always be dedicated.

Before I let you move on, it's important to note a few things. I assume you've read book 1 since you're here, ready to uncover more of Sunlatveria. The foundations of these stories go back years, built in my mind to perfume what was. While Edwins initial landing party was full of German sailors and researchers, the great worldwide migration of World War One quickly diversified the island. In our world today, one broken solely on the backs of undeserved hate and misunderstanding, it's also important to remember each of us contain inside the will to do good and the potential to be great. While evil and darkness lurk inside all men, we can overcome and dispel these demons with a little faith and willpower.

The Lightning Eater

Book 2:

The Edge of Sanctuary

By Brett T. Hebrank II

Art Provided by Saad Ali

in cooperation with

Archmage Industrious (www.mage-in.com)

This is a work of fiction. Pure fiction. If any names, locations or events coincide with any real persons, places or events, such is from pure coincidence.

Chapter 1

The Smoldering Spot

"What can I do, for you?" Quietly sings a young Harold into the emptiness, staring dreamily across a classroom of about fifty other immigrant and ethnic teenagers, his internal sights locked on a dark-haired girl near the door. The unnamed female, sits with her legs crossed tightly in a flowing black sundress, bent over as she scribbles insanely into a notebook. The three students that surround her engage in irrelevant discussion, choosing rather to chat than to absorb the scientific teachings of an old balding Caucasian in a dingy brown suit droning on in a boring tirade of misinformation and uselessness.

“What can I do, that no one else can do?” Harold whispers again, all sense pointed at the mysterious girl still scribbling wildly in her notebook. He thinks hard trying to remember her name, it was only day three of his ninth year in school, each class went through a series of icebreakers and other torturous rounds of ‘hello, my name is…’, he figured she must’ve said her name at least once. As his mind wanders, the tedious speaker at the front of the class addresses the chittering group surrounding the unnamed girl.

“Why don’t you four just pipe down before I dismiss you from this class completely!?” He breaks from his sleep-inducing tone now enforcing his word with a much stronger and hardened appeal. Stepping towards the adolescents as they scurry back into their front-facing, backs straightened upright positions, the unnamed girl, unfortunately grouped with the talkative trio, continues to scribble unpassed as if not a single word drifted into her ear canal.

“Miss Haze?” The professor is now directly in front of her desk, standing over her as she continues to sketch, the sounds of her scribbling grows obnoxiously louder as the classroom focuses on the disrespectful youth in the front.

“Just one second.” A dim golden aura shines from her pecan-colored skin as she speaks up loud to soft.

Harold winces as he hears her innocent voice, her childish tone knocks loose the memory of her introducing herself days ago.

"Dolores Haze!" Harold says aloud in exuberant joy, his voice carrying heavy throughout the class and the focus shifts to him. He begins to shiver nervously as the professor looks his way.

"Anything you'd like to add mister... What was it again?" The teacher asks again in his monotone voice, each syllable looser than the last. Harold grips the sides if the desk in front of him, mouth open as his brain struggles to find any words that present an ounce of sense. Haze looks up from her mysteriously important drawing and joins the class in awe at the illness of Harold's outburst. Yet, through the blurred faces of the multicultural class, he manages to lock eyes with the clear bronze faced Haze, hair in two long black ponytails. She was beyond any human he'd ever and found himself stuck in the stare.

"Nothing sir." Harold manages to say in a firmer voice than his own, releasing the sweat-soaked wood as his eyes stay on Dolores. A smile forms on her face from the initial smirk of confusion presented by the teacher, who heads back to the chalkboard to continue his lecture. The two sit in the warm glow of the others smiling gaze for another minute before she turns back to the front, continuing to smile to herself.

....

My eyes shoot open as the seven A.M. bells go off outside. I sit up from the thick white satin comforter blanket, rubbing away the sleep from my eyes as i slide my legs of the bed. Peggy lies still asleep on the other side the unnecessarily large bed. The floor is a heated white and black-stained marble floor, with a shine so intense one could stare into the floor and see the ceiling and back again until there were no more reflections to see.

I make my way over to the patio door and head out onto the balcony, some days I'd head to the ledge and look over my father's garden before heading into his neurotic screenplay called 'life in Sunlatveria as the founders' son. I step through the shimmering crystal bead-door imported from Belize and onto the terrace of unrivaled creation and precipitousness. It's not until I reach the banister overlooking the massive enclosure of green, that I feel my father's energy behind me, sitting just to the right of the double doors into my bedroom in the wooden rocking chair sent from my aunt back in New York.

"Father." I turn around briskly leaning back onto the carved-stone bannister, he sits back with his left foot atop his right knee, reading a German newspaper and taking light tokes from a thick cigar pinched in between his shining white teeth.

"Good morning." I add as he turns a page without looking up to me.

"When is she going home?" He asks finally looking up to me as he takes his cigar and extends it through the support beams of the bannister to ash the behemoth.

"When she's ready to leave." I exclaim without hesitation, expecting him to rebuttal with forty-seven reasons why she had to go.

"Look son, I can give you fifty reasons why you need to send her back to New York immediately." I roll my eyes in astonished surprise, he takes notice.

"But I won't." He adds as he begins to fold up the paper, the cigar is back hanging out of his mouth like a limp bratwurst.

"Instead you'll lecture me about the finer points of romance? Listen Edwin, I don't need love advice from someone who abandoned their wife to continue his little sailing adventure. Why don't you focus less on molding me and head over to the council and do a better job governing the island you founded, instead of lounging in you dark cave all day long. You're the head governing entity in this county and you prance around like your priorities lie elsewhere, like the rest of the world isn't on the verge of global conflict that could possibly find its way here to where you have us calling home!" I turn around in a huff of unvented anguish, arms crossed I gaze across the multiple sections of the multi-pathed garden. I can feel the air pressure change as he rises from his seat and walks closer to me, stopped about halfway between the chair and where I stand.

"Meet me in the throne room in one hour Harold." He says in a rushed tone, as if he could no longer be in a dialogue with a lesser being such as me. I feel his presence dissipate and diminish as a bright flash illuminates from behind me. An extraordinary light beyond anything found anywhere else on Earth, I'd become too accustomed to the fading shadow of wild energies and unsurpassed electricity. I turn around to a still-lit cigar slowly drifting on the glassy stone porch, sizzling glitters of spark and light descending slowly from the sky.

I'd only been on the island six months before the initial bliss faded. Edwin started forcing me to attend his council meetings with him, forcing me into a role I'd never intended upon. As he drags we across the island for store openings, town hall conferences and council meetings, I started to see the love he felt for this land and its people. And the people showed their gratitude in return, but it's hard for the Vizanti council to noticeably contain their resentment of him. I tell him constantly but he dismisses my opinion, perhaps he knows of their true agendas for I can only speculate theories for now.

The awakening smell of the garden is lessened by the tobacco stuffed cigar that I am forced to remove in a violent huff that is interrupted mid-kick by an ear-drumming crack of thunder that booms overhead. I catch my balance as the thunder strike fades and I move towards the bedroom stepping over the now dim cigar.

Through the door I make my way over to a still sleep Peggy Shaw. I take a seat next to her sleeping on her side, stopping for a moment to take in the curves of her face and cheeks. A sight I wouldn't get to enjoy again for an indefinite amount of time, due to retrogressive garbage disguised as politics that my father can't seem to rebuff. I focus back of her near-flawless ebony skin as her wide sunny eyes whisper open. The angel of Venus sits up against the large specialty-carved oak backboard rubbing the dream from her face revealing a sunnier undercoat.

"Good morning love." I say softly moving a stream of hair from her face and tucking it behind her ear.

"Good morning sunshine." She says ecstatically yet soft in a dreamy voice as she grabs my hand gently and kiss my wrist. "So I hear it's time for me to get moving'?" She says jokingly, lightly pecking up and down my forearm.

"You heard?" I say as my hand falls gently against her hair like a still waterfall. "I didn't mean to wake you up

"I was awaken when you lifted from the bed, besides It's not like the thunder wasn't going to wake me up anyway. I will never get used to that... Or any of this to be completely honest with you Harry. I mean, you're like some sort of modern day prince, with family drama that rivals the stories of old." She looks wide-eyed at me as I stare back in amusement and comfort.

"The stories of old?" I ask interested as I begin to move over her legs and into the wild blankets beside her.

"Yeah, ancient religions, mythologies that sort of stuff. I really got into this Greek Mythology phase of my life." She putter slowly between sentences, slightly embarrassed from what I could only assume was her reading extensively into a long absent religion, a fact that only increased my infatuation. "Apollo, Poseidon, Hades, Aphrodite, Theseus, Percyu-, Percy, Persus-._ She stops to think, sitting forward with her legs crossed beneath the colors.

"Perseus." I say rubbing her shoulders terribly attempting to massage her.

"Yeah that's it, besides the point your father is, the main guy, what was his name again?" She sits back turning to face me as I adjust with my back against the headboard to face her.

"Jupiter is for the Romans so the answer must be Zeus." I answer smiling as I start to subconsciously into her lustrous dark shell. "Zeus! Yes! Then that means you're Achilles, Hercules, Perseus or Pollux."

"Its interesting that you remember all the demigod sons of Zeus but you stumbled on Zeus himself." I ask jokingly smiling as i wrap my arms around her, she reciprocates.

"Take your pick." She says softly as she starts to kiss my arm hugged over her chest.

"That's the thing though Peg." I say kissing the top of her head before moving towards the edge of the bed. "Edwin's not Zeus, he's Chronos." I add as my romanticized internal theme fades and the usual rampant flood of anxiety and aversion swell within me. Softly I toss her all-white suitcase onto the bed and begin to heartlessly gather her things from across the room onto a makeshift pile near her feet.

"Your father will never approve of us, I'm starting to think it's race related, or is he just another misogynistic Aryan with a god complex?" Peggy questions as she proceeds to get dressed.

"I'm still struggling to understand the man, but I'm sure a racist is one thing he isn't, he's told me multiple time all human life started in Africa for one and I mean c'mon Sunlatveria is one of the most multicultural places in the world right now, next time you visit I'm taking you to Cobain Square and you'll see, it's better than New York." Giddily i finish getting dressed, tossing on whatever items of clothing are nearest while trying to maintain a solid color scheme of black.

"Well I'd love to move here and be with you full-time if it wasn't for your beloved father personally blocking my citizen request." Fixing her hair in the mirror she pauses to stare at my reflection. "You say it's nothing against my skin color, right? Then tell me what is it about me that he finds so utterly repelling that he won't allow me here when all I want is your happiness. I've known you longer than he has, I should have some rank in your life Harry." She starts to cry lightly, eyes still locked on mine.

My mind struggles to come up with any words of comfort so in silence I approach her and sit my hands on her shoulders. She turns back to the vanity mirror bordered in white wicker and begins to clean up her face. Her tears subside as I kiss her once on the head, her head smelling heavy of lavender and peaches. She smiles and in silence still I turn back towards the other half of the room to finish getting myself ready for the day.

"I love you Peg. You just have to trust me. I have a bad feeling about this place." I turn back towards her still at the door.

"Oh Harold." She approaches me, plants a kiss on my cheek and continues back to the bathroom without saying another word.

Minutes later she is dressed in dark blue garments and a silk black scarf covers her lower face. I can't help but to compliment her taste in color and cloth, and after a quick thank you peck on the cheek we make our way out of my room and down the main staircase towards the driveway. A car still waiting for us at the palace gate, two stone pillars each 15 meters high and a metal banner that read one word 'choose' surrounded by fancy metal-crafting artwork. My arm wrapped around her waist we make our way down the cobblestone driveway towards the large arching metal gates, each branded with a large 'S' surrounded by seemingly vague animalistic artwork.

The entrance sat across two separate bridges, each eighty to ninety meters long and another forty in width, away from the palace that sat alone on the most inner Solitude Lake island.

I open the car door as a gentleman should, and after helping Peggy into the vehicle I rush to the other side to place her bags beside her, again I rush back to the other side to say goodbye.

"Now when you get back to the States call me okay." I say worriedly before kissing her on the forehead. She smiles and grabs my collar as I pull away, pulling me back in for a kiss proportional in passion to the distance she'd have to travel. After a few moments I pull away again and again she stops me.

"I'll see you soon Harry, you be safe alright?" She asks inquisitively.

"Of course Peg, I love you, have a safe journey." I kiss her again on the lis before pulling out of the taxi window and backing away from the curb.

"I love you." She says before the glass window begins to raise an the car pulls away.

I watch the car disappear around a bend before pulling out a pre-rolled joint from my inner jacket pocket and a pack of matches. As I proceed back towards the house I light the cigarette, taking light breathes and I scan the scenic serenity of Solitude Island as I cross the bridges over the shimmering waters.

Solitude provides with a breathtaking view no matter where you look. As I continue towards the garage up the driveway, the chitter of birds in the trees gets louder. The crashing of the waves onto the rocky shores of the palace island beat gently from all over and the air is heavy with the scent of freshly planted flowers. The garden brims with greenery of all sorts, yet I continue up the stained cobblestone towards the wood-paneling garage door, which now begins to open explicitly.

A darker man steps out from under the slowing rising door about four meters wide, he was donned in a freshly pressed, yellow and brown pin stripped suit.

"Uh...Hello?" I ask curiously approaching the door, stopping right in the front the man adjusting his suit. "Who are you?" I add brazenly. He slicks back his hair and smiles while extending a hand, he reeked of lily and sweat despite his face being dry.

"Excuse me ol' chap, names Allen Parker." He reaches out a hand in greeting. "You must be Harold, oh I've heard so much about you my boy." He laughs wholly with his hand on his stomach. "Bloody nice day isn't it Harry? This is why I fell in love with this place, the beautiful weather. My sinuses' have never been clearer." He begins to brush past me, rambling incoherently about the humidity and the cloud participation. Confused, I turn and continue back into the garage towards one of the back corners.

I hop on one of my father's bicycles and begin pedaling down the driveway at a leisurely speed, expecting to past the mysterious Englishman. I stop once I've cross the bridge completely, the road splits in three directions from here, forest and mountain cover ever horizon as the sun shines brightly overhead. The serene beauty of the island overtakes me for a moment and I forget my objectives completely. After a while I come to my senses through the cackling of the bird overhead and I continue down the marked roads, following the signs to Theseus, on the outskirts of which I'd find the Vizanti Hall, the meeting place for the Sunlatverian government.

The ride is smooth, bumpy in some areas but the magnificence of the environment makes up for the sore behind. Between the giant Oak and Redwoods that don't belong and the colorful rows of mismatching flowers and various crop fields that again, didn't belong. Edwin claims when he found the island, he thought he was dreaming, fauna and flora packed to the canopy. Animal and plant hybrids that would make Gregor Mendal faint on sight. On closer inspection with a few plants, such as tulips, you can see veins of blue electricity within the plants otter stem walls, it's a gorgeous sight, Mom even keeps a fresh bouquet of her favorite flowers in the kitchen at all times.

Soon, I find myself on the outskirts of Theseus, a small Northern township right on the coast built around the Vizanti Hall. The town resembles pictures I'd seen of villages from Northern Europe. Gas lamps line the edges of the stained blue cobblestone streets as the towns inhabits bustle about, following their individual daily routines of shopping, eating, working and lounging. A streetcar or two whizz by as I continue peddling along the right side of the road, the hall coming into view just over some apartment buildings ahead.

I pass a fruit and vegetables shop with the windows recently busted out, the owner still picking up boxes and litter inside. I park the bike against the building and offer to help him clean without introducing myself asking what has happened. He explains briefly that there a group of Aryans terrorizing new immigrants throughout this district. I comfort him and reassure him these men will be found and that their actions are against the will of the island. He smiles before going back to his rearranging as I begin sweeping up glass. After a bit, I notice my sisters Louise and Abigail peeking through a store window across the street, before long they spot me and move across the street.

“Hey Harry.” Excitedly screams my younger sister Abigail, jetting toward me for a hug, her grasp around my torso has always the been the tightest.

“Hey little sister.” I say softly smiling down at her as I hug her back. My eyes drift close in the ruffling of her deep brown hair, kept at bay from her face by a single light blue headband about an inch wide. When my eyes open again, I find myself staring face to face with my estranged sister Louise. She glares back at me with a smug veil concealing her contempt for me.

"Harold, morning." She says politely out of obligation stepping up the steep curb.

"Louise, good morning. Where are you two headed?" I ask as Abi finally loosens her grip and rushes over to the large store window when Louise arms crossed in horror.

"What happened here?" She asks me before considering the shop and running to check on the clerk, I yell behind her continuing to clean, explaining the same story he'd told before. I finish up cleaning the store front as Louise gathers the business man's information and before long were back on the street. Abigail pulls me across the street to the window they stood at before I arrived.

"Lulu was taking me shopping for school clothes and I saw this pretty vase for mother." Lulu was Abigails pet name for Louise, back in New York Abigail was too young to make friends of her own and with me going from school to work and back again, I could never really be the big brother she needed sometimes. Louise was a few years older than I, but despite her unpronounced resentment of me, she loves Abigail as much as anyone would love their younger sibling.

"Which one?" I set the bicycle against the wall and get closer to the freshly-cleaned glass.

"That one, with the purple flowers." She points at a bright white porcelain vase, hand-painted with thick layers of purple and indigo flowers that seemed to burst from the two-dimensional plane.

"I think she'd like it Abigail." I agree putting my hands in my pockets as Louise turns towards the glass, now the three of us lined in height gawk in the store window with me the middle. The sign just above reads: Allens Antiques.

"Oh yes, how could I forget..." Louise speaks up turning towards me with her hands still clasped. "Aren't you supposed to be meeting father at the Hall." She finishes.

"Yes. Yes yes yes." I ramble, my eyes now wandering throughout the store, expecting something to jump out and catch my eye. I'd spent all my life living at the bottom, working every day after school to help my mom feed, heat, cloth me and my baby sister. Now that I've inherited my fathers legacy, his money, his island his power; I find myself lost, perhaps now more than I've ever been. A few seconds of silence pass as I continue to stall, now wondering how Louise knew where I headed.

"So. Are you going to get moving or shall I go in your steed?" Louise asks arrogantly smirking back through the store window.

"Louise if I didn't know any better I'd say you resented me ever coming to this island." A confused rush of emotion boils over in my chest, outside I maintain a confident aura despite the feeling of dread creeping up my esophagus.

"Harry don't be like that." Abigail speaks up, pulling my wrist out of my pocket. Louise pulls out of dark purple coin purse from her jacket inner pocket and hands it to Abigail.

"Abi, run in the store and ask the nice woman behind the counter to get that vase for Mal wrapped, okay?" Louise politely commands Abi, smiling happily she skips off into the store, once immediately in, Lou turns back to me, her facing warping back to the stale static I'd grown fond of.

"Shame, I enjoy seeing you smile and grin, seeing your teeth and gums really brightens my day Lou." I attempt to make her smile again playfully, but her smiles are reserved for a lucky few and I have never seemed to be one with luck.

"Harold, how about you cut the manure. You're god damn right I have a problem with you, I've had a problem since the day I first heard you're pathetic name. You Americans are all dirty hill-people, incapable of running government, incapable of showing compassion, incapable of seeing the blasted forest! Only ever seeing a single leaf." She's ready to keep going, perhaps for hours but I interrupt rudely.

"What about that kiss?" I ask, remembering my first day on the island when she forced herself on me just outside of my fathers throne room.

"It was a bloody test you imbecile! I've spent the last two decades preparing to take this island from my beloved father when he passes. To move this government into an age beyond any nation on earth!" She pauses, staring off over the hoards of passing citizens.

"This is my home Harold. No one is more equipped to lead than I, no one knows it better. I was my fathers light, for years it was just him and me. Yeah Ali was there, but I taught her English and soon we became this sort of weird makeshift family." She pauses again, this time looking towards a giddy Abigail inside, chatting it up with the saleswoman as she gracefully packages the vase in a bright green box. I am left speechless in her purge.

"I guess it's not all bad. I mean... you're not that bad Harold. It's just disappointing, I'd thought father was this revolutionary, this visionary, this... godly creature. And then I find out. After years of looking up to him, that he's just as misogynistic as the rest of man. Which in my head, proves to me that he is unworthy of the throne upon which he sits."

"I'm sorry I cant relate to this prejudice, and I apologize for pushing you out of fathers light. To be truthful I don't want it, never did. I only came to this... wickedly vile place to fetch my mother." The words 'wickedly vile" spew from my mouth like flies from a field, a falsehood both of us could see right through.

"Vile huh?" She laughs for a second, smiling as she moves my head upward by my chin. "Cheer up little brother, now that you know my angst against you, maybe we ca be friends now. I'd been holding that in for a while."

"Since the second he said my name huh?" I ask jokingly smiling back towards Abigail moving towards the exit, still laughing with the clerk.

"It's in the past, and while father still aggravates me heavily with his newfound persona, I do believe there is still hope for you, there is time for you to learn, an eagerness to evolve." She smiles poking me in the stomach.

"And that kiss, you said you were testing me?" I add before Abigail opens the shop door.

"It's also in the past, and it'll never happen again. Wow, is that all that's on your minds? Silly man, trapped in his cycle of primal urges and superiority complexes. Abi! Are you ready for the next stop on our tour?"

"Absolutely!" Abi grins hard as the large box now wrapped in brown paper slowly slips form her hand. Louise catches it before it touches the ground, deciding to hold it for her until they got home.

"You need to be more careful Abi, just because you have a big sister doesn't change anything, do you remember what I used to say every morning before I left back home?" I hop on the bicycle preparing to ride off.

"Trust no one." Abigail says tediously in her crackling pre-teen voice, as if she'd said it a thousand times and was growing weary.

"That's right, trust no one. Except of course Lulu here, she is the only exception alright?" I exclaim jokingly as I extend myself over the handle bars towards Abigail.

"Right." Abigail responds.

"Don't worry about the ladies Harry, go on, father and his Council of Trent await." Louise wraps her free arm around Abi and they start down the path.

"Council of Trent?" I ask quietly to myself. I begin peddling toward the large obelisk looking auditorium hall looming under the beating sun. Mentally I repeat 'Council of Trent' over and over until I reach the hall, to remember the phrase so research can be done later in the library. Let's just say the American educational system was on a different path than the rest of the worlds, Sunlatveria included. I can recite all the presidents up until now, and all the states even the newer ones. If it wasn't for the few years of university that I received, I'd be stuck as one of those dim-witted people that legitimately believe the Earth is not a sphere or how precipitation works. I'd finally reached Vizanti hall, smaller up close than when I first entered town. At only about three stories tall, the hall was rectangular and modeled after Ancient Greco architecture, tall pillars across the front entrance, glassless windows cut delicately into the stone scatter the flat sides of the oddly shaped mass.

The individual blocks seemed to glow bright white in the sun, despite their rusted gold brushing. Sunlatveria flags and guardsmen decorate the front entrance. Nonchalantly I drop my fathers bicycle against the warm pavement of the curved driveway before headed inside passed the two guards posted just outside the main doors. I nod slightly towards the right guard, a pale hulking man with his eyes stuck forward and his hands frozen at his sides. Onward into the hall I press and moments later, through several fancy wooden doors, I find myself the center of attention in a room filled with old greying politicians and businessmen alike.

"Late, again. What a surprise. Is this really your choice of heir, Hebrank? Boy this country is really going to have it rough." Says a familiar contemptuous Russian. "The girl would have been much better, served all of our purposes much better." He laughs to himself as the rest of the room quietly stares back and forth between him, me and my father seated at the other end of the room. About thirty-five people sat around the ye-shaped table, with father seated just as the angled end, facing towards me will wrought colored across his face.

"Harold take a seat beside me." He motions towards the empty chair beside him. The concrete minimalist décor of the room felt cold, a vast contrast against the bright gold and green bannering scattered about.

“Let me wash up father, I’ll only be a minute.” I stutter jogging lightly to quiet my steps in the echoing chamber as the delegates of the council stare judgmentally onward.

I scurry down an odd angled hall towards the lavatories when I see her, Ali, smoking a cigarette and sitting in a low window with her feet dangling inside. Her sundress, a deep yellow, bristles lightly in the windows breeze, a white bow around her waist and a white sleeve top showing off her glowing natural tan in the sun.

“Harry!” She says in an excited but satirical tone. “What brings you to this dreadful hall of dialogue and progress.” I past the washroom door and casually lean against the window sidepane with a hand in my pocket, with the other I snatch the cigarette from her mouth.

“Same as you I suppose, just another pet in Edwins collection.” I joke taking a quick drag, gazing out the window for a moment as I the cigarette back, stuck for a second on the view.

“You don’t know him like I do, you apart of his personal entourage now.” She laughs before taking her cigarette back, her fingers drag slowly across my skin as she pulls away.

"Well I hope I get treated better than family." I grunt looking back over at her.

"Edwin is fickle, he's a generally considerate individual, it's the council I'm concerned about." She explains taking short drags from the almost out cigarette. "He treats his family well Harry, if he'd known about you sooner…"

"Don't do that Ali." I interrupt, it's a sob story I've heard too many times back in the States every time someone found out my dad was dead. "Just don't try to justify him or that act."

"What?! Leaving you and your mother to sail comfortably alone to the United States? As he ventured into a hurricane in the name of higher science?" She flicks the cigarette and gives me cold stare.

I can only give her the same stare of dense contemplation. I sigh, lost in the washy depths of her glazy colored eyes, the wind lightly bristling the tips of her hair.

"Every time I'm with you we only seem to discuss my father, his ideals, his cohorts, his colleagues." I pause as her eyes connect with mine, curiosity yet cautious blushes across her face.

"You don't know what he has done to this place, and in such a short time, he's not only civilized energy itself, but he's given millions of immigrants and refugees homes in the last twenty years." She swivels in her seat, her legs now dangling out of the window just inches above a blooming bush covered in daisies. "You need to get past your personal baggage if you're ever going to do what needs to be done Harold."

"Personal baggage?" I step forward, crossing my arms in disbelief. "I just wanted to talk about something other than Edwin Ali is that so much to..." Mid-sentence she leaps from the window, pushing herself off the wall and somersaulting over the daisy bush. Standing, she turns to me and waves before leaping over the seven-foot-high brick wall that enclosed the governing hall. She was so graceful, the two flips seemed to flow seamlessly into all her motions. She moved so effortlessly as she disappeared over the wall.

"Are you coming?" I hear her yell form over the wall, at the same time I hear footsteps coming down the hall. Someone heavy moving from the main conference room.

"Definitely." I thought as I vaulted out of the window, narrowly missing the delicate flowers and landing in the side yard. Unable to leap over the wall, I just kind of crept my way towards the front courtyard where I see Ali, well at least her legs. I slowly crept towards her fine legs poking out from the driver side door of fancy sports mobile.

"Looking for the keys?" I ask as I crouch behind the car facing the hall.

"Who needs 'em" She says as she sticks her head, smiling at me as the automobile spurts alive. "Hop in kid." She jokes as she climbs into the driver's seat.

"Ya' know, we never discussed how old you are." I make conversation as I climb into the passenger side. "I mean what, you're Edwins. bodyguard? Wife? Servant? I'm just saying is you look only a few years older than me." She accelerates and exits the compound, working the steering wheel like a professional. "He said he found you here, a native, but you don't seem like any native I'd ever seen."

"Have you seen any natives before" She asks looking at me over her arm high as she maneuvers around a tight corner. "In New York?"

"No, but I've seen some moving pictures, read a few textbooks."

"Just say no, alright?" She sighs as I agree. "My integration into the modern world should serve as some example to your fathers will. The lake kept me healthy alright, healthy and young and strong and able. Before your father came I was already a force to be reckoned with, just feral. Edwin and Louise worked tirelessly to teach me English, German, French and Russian. On top of that they gave me a family, something I had to realize I was without for a long time."

"How long?" I interrupt as her voice starts to crack.

"What?" She replies lightly tearing up under her left eye.

"How old are you? How long were you out there alone?" My arm rest on the open window sill, my eyes locked on her, the passing scenery behind her like one of those faux backgrounds from the films.

"Not sure Harry, why does it matter?" She wipes her face, shooting me a brief smile before upturning into New High.

"The people wanna know." I joke looking out of the window. This was my first time in New High since I arrived.

"One things for sure." She says smiling normally again, driving with one hand as she slows near a curb.

"Yeah? Whats that?" I ask.

"Your little sister sure loves you." The car slows to a halt as I see what sees smiling about, Abigail and Louise standing on the side of the road, both with a handful of bags each.

We both hop out of the car as Abi runs to hug me, then Ali next as Louise follows suite nonchalantly.

The girls all begin chatting as we form a company near the curb, the conversation begins to drone in the background as I look around the city street, clean from gutter to rooftop. It was a familiar sight, reminiscent of our neighborhood in South Brooklyn, only nicer, more extravagant with each building sports its own unique mineral material and coloring, no two skyscrapers stood the same. Shops and restaurants line both sides of the thruway, with a large arcade banner hanging over a festive courtyard in front of a few of the storefronts. A large fountain sat in the middle of the maybe one hundred meters across courtyard, busy with shoppers, travelers and citizens alike. Oriental music buzzing from a nearby due planted on a rug near the center fountain. The air heavy with the smell of fried foods and baked delicacies from around the world.

The group focuses to me, with Louise shaking me lightly by the shoulder to wake up.

"Are you well brother?" Louise says softly as my eyes swing back onto the girls huddled around me in caution.

"Yeah...Yes of course, just taking in the sights. Its beyond beautiful." I exclaim, still scanning the unique and fabulous architecture of the city's design.

"It is something else..." Louise agrees smiling and sighing as her eyes drift behind me. Caution again drifts across her face as her eyes lock on some commotion happening behind us near the entrance to a yellow bricked building, framed with shining white marble. "What's going on here?" She says calmly as Ali and Abigail begin to stare inquisitively and intensely at the scene unfolding.

Behind me I hear a lot of screaming in German, followed by muffled whimpering in German, English and French. I turn to see a large circle forming around what seems to be three or four men dancing around in a circle. We approach dutifully, gently pushing through the crowd until the four of us were at the edge of what turned out to be a horrific scene of ignorance and unjustified hatred.

At first I see the horrified couple, a bloodied Caucasian man, short cut hair wearing a white button up with the sleeve rolled up with black slacks. Desperately he clings to a dark skin woman with her long jet black hair ruffled and covered in filth from the sidewalk, she appears to be only in her under most garments. Above them, four varying in size and height Caucasian men dance around them, switching savagely between dancing and laughing to beating the couple with assorted items of torturous hate.

The largest, a tall balding man with a brown handlebar mustache, strikes the French speaking man with a two and a half foot long skinny tree branch. The Frenchman muffles his pain as he attempts to shield his love at all cost. She, barely conscience attempts to call for help in German, English, and French, in hopes someone would end their suffering. The remaining men used a combinations of leather belts and loose horse strappings. The crowd that engulfed us was mix of horrified people, scared to react, and a few cheering from their dark corners of anonymity.

“STOP!!!” A dark skin man rushes through the crowd and falls to the ground near the couple, crying and weeping softly as he runs his hands across both the man and woman, both breathing heavily. The outburst causes the attackers to stop their merriment for a moment, their focus now shifting to the interrupter.

"Get out of here baboon." One of the attackers says, cracking a dusty leather belt as he slowly circles the trio on the pavement. "Less we move you up on the list."

"Someone get the constable!" I hear someone yell from behind.

"How about you settle down." Louise steps forward. "How about we all calm down here." Her voice booming over the scene, the attacker's attention has been shifted to us. I can hear a sigh of relief float from the kneeling brown shirted man over the lying couple.

"Hey you." Ali says, trying to whisper to the keeling man. "Get to out of here and to some help immediately." He turns to us, his eyes a light green weeping heavily and a star of David dangling around his neck, he nods thankfully.

The attackers watch as they approach us in a line, attempting to intimidate the two women had just spoken up against them.

"German immigrant I suppose?" Louise jokes casually to the silent men staring us down.

"Henrik's a Serb." The middle, and largest says pointing over his left shoulder to the smallest henchman, smiling manically with his chin up. “But that doesn’t matter, he sees same vision as us.” His English is choppy but good enough.

“Ja, same vision, Aryan race is master race.” The other German speaks up, cracking his knuckles as he stares down Louise. Just then, a flash of incredible light blinds us and the attackers from above.

As the whiteness begins the fade, the dramatic burst is followed by a roaring crack of thunder, nearly deafening the remaining crowd. After the initial yet familiar fear subsided, I sighed in relief as I opened my eyes fully. There stood Edwin, now draped in some oddly fashioned black thin plate armor and a dark cape that hung just inches from the ground, the inside of the cape was the same dark blue that run underneath the entirety of his suit. He stood there in this fantastical new suit, hugging Louise first and foremost.

“Father, this suit, what is this?” I step forward impressed by the outfit that seemed to allow plenty of mobility despite the thick black plates.

“Later Harold.” He says to me with a light smile before moving his focus back to Louise.

“Someone explain what’s going on here.” Edwin’s speaks aloud as he drifts his head back, still grasping Louise who is almost as tall as him.

"High Chancellor!" The leading attacker's steps forward to speak up. "Please let me."

"Father no!" Abigail cries out from behind me.

"Abigail!" Edwin screams. "You'll have your turn." He turns back to the sweat covered man and nods for him to speak.

"High chancellor. Me and my fellow compatriots were only providing a free service to you and your establishment. We were on the verge of finishing some… "He smirks suspiciously. "…Harrowing business, when these adolescents interrupted our session."

"And what business might you be providing us, Mister…?" Edwin replies, finally releasing Louise who falls back in line with us. The crowd behind us more silent than ever, watching in awe and interest.

"Richter sir, well to be frank, we've been riding your island of inferior species since we arrived several weeks ago. This couple here." Pointing away. "Should be burned at the stake, Jewish Frenchman takes an African whore as his wife, what fiction. We correct such errors in your flags name." The man folds his arms in confidence as Edwin's face drifts into the thick crowd of onlookers, he stops at a gap in the mass. I turn to see the interracial couple lying on the ground a couple of yards from where I last saw them. From there I could tell the man had succumbed to his injuries, a doctor was attempting to fix up the woman as strangers bring an assortment of water and blankets. The dark shirted man still weeping over his injured loved one.

Edwin looks around the crowd again before falling his eyes on us, his legacy. He steps towards us, his cape swinging as he turns.

"Louise, I'll be headed to Europe for few weeks. Get to the Vizanti Hall, run the Capital until I get back please darling." He says softly before kissing his near the left ear. She nods in agreement as he moves over to Ali.

"My dearest, please take Abigail home to her mother. Remember what we talked about, I be back in due time." He kisses her on the opposite cheek.

"Of course, my love." She nods smiling as she grabs Abigail's hand.

"Stay nearby my love, Harold will be with you soon." Edwin adds as Ali nods again, taking Abigail through the parting crowd, we all watch in unison as they disappear into a nearby deli. The staff. Now a part of the curious crowd, rushes back into the store to get everything prepared for the royal family's impromptu visit. The crowds focus shifts back to Edwin, the three tittering attackers and me.

"High Chancellor!" The speaker for the men speaks up again, this time yelling with a highly disrespectful tone.

"What now sire? You glide in from the heavens, a perfect image of our shared homeland." He crosses his arms, lightning smirking as his eyes start to devilishly glance past all the faces of the ethically ambiguous crowd. "What now magician? Are we free to, as the travel guides say, express ourselves freely? Or are you another lying piece of trash, sprouting endlessly about politics and magical powers? You have your aboriginal." Glancing towards Ali with a serpentine smile.

"Let us get ours." He motions towards the immolated martyrs and the brutish thug then takes a step towards Edwin. My father looks down before turning to face me, his eyes dart over to the victims, then back to me. The unthinking ruffian opens his mouth to speak again when Edwin throws his right hand into the air breaking the still silence of the bazaar's masses, his fingers spread wide with the sun glinting wildly off his plated gauntlets. He commences to rotate with his eyes closed, drawing the full attention of the crowd.

As if to speak, he opens his mouth taking in ample air and he stops rotating just as his shoulders become parallel with mine. His mouth closes as he lowers his head, his eyes beginning to burn a bright white despite them being closed. Still stiff and straightened he drops his arm and above us three columns of lightning burst through a thicket of clouds, descending rapidly. Before the bystanders and ignorant Neanderthals have a chance to react, the columns slim into three precious dagger-shaped objects with unstable trails of blue electricity and white flames. Like cannonballs sent from Zeus, the bolts liquidate the three brutes in a flash of light that blinds most of the onlookers cowering for cover.

The lamb stand frozen between arrant mystification and inexpressible terror as each receives their very own damnation, striking through every cell, burning every molecule until they were nothing. In a monstrous display of excessive brutality, the lightning rips the men to pieces and the explosion splatters bits of carnage into every direction.

His hand falls completely to his side, somehow Edwin is untouched by the horror, only a bit of char is seen on his fluttering two-tone cape. Without turning back to the crater of guts and bone, he approaches me, grabbing my shoulder he turns me from the remnants of the horrific scene and he guides me into the parting crowd of shocked faces, towards where Ali dragged the curious Abigail.

"Wait, I should say something." Edwin says aloud before turning back to the crowd, still frozen in waning silence. Again, he throws his hands into the air, accidently spooking the already agitated crowd.

"My People!!!" His gruff voice booms over the entire market square, he proceeds to walk towards the smoldering impact zone, lowering his hands as the multitudes again come to a standstill.

"Sons and daughter of Sunlatveria, listen!" His silvery voice carries across the street as more citizens begins to flood from the various buildings,

“I will not always be here, to draw the lines of what is acceptable and what is not!” He puts his hands behind him as he approaches an apple truck near some fruit stands.

“The future of this country is not in my hands.” He climbs atop the apple crate in the pickup so he can overlook the crowd, now gathered around him. The burnt impact crater disappears as the crowd moves forward.

“The future of this country rest in your hands. What happened today, is wrong. Let it be known, it matters not what you believe, your pigment, where you are from or whatever measly rival your old families are caught in. It matters not who you pray to in the night, or better yet what you see as pleasure in the night. We are all family here. All humans, from China to Norway we are all cousins. We are all one species, trust me I have seen it. Together we can rise, separated we all fall.” He pauses looking down at me for a moment before continuing.

“The rising fascist powers in Europe aim to cleanse their continent of all those they see as inferior. This is what they believe to be right, and they are willing to burn the entire world to accomplish their goals. Next to these powers we have other entities attempting to convert all life on Earth, turning innocence into hatred, nature into war, history into fuel. Sunlatveria has grown exponentially due to the Great War, the great Migration of millions of people. Immigrants, refugees, deserters from every corner of the globe somehow found this land and soon they came to call it home. We here, will remain free from the haunting touch of conflict, will keep our bounders open, we will provide a refuge, a haven for the downtrodden and displaced. But as far as international policy is concerned, we will have zero relations, zero discussions with any outside entity. While the first war hardened out edges, I will not allow a second to bring us to the brink." The crowd grasps at the thought of another conflict as destructive as the Great War. "Yes, another war looms, one possibly far more destructive than any conflict humans have seen thus far." He clears his throat, the sun reflecting off his darkened chest plate.

"Today, I shall be departing to Europe, I aim to snuff the growing flames of ignorance. The hatred you've witnessed today, was birthed in the heart of my own fatherland." He sighs heavily, taking his eyes to the ground before rising them again.

"Therefore, I feel some responsibility in ending this evil before it spreads, corrupting the world for centuries. This is home to me now, make it home to you as well and together we shall protect this land. We will prosper here. We will thrive and I swear to all of you here today..." He puts his hands up again over the crowd. "The lightning will forever protect us!" the crowd begins to cheer in awe as streaks of lightning swirl in the sky above, spinning the fluffy white coluds into a vortex as the bolts danced. The columns sizzled white as sparks and embers of blue and purple fell from the tornado a thousand miles above our heads. He looks down at me as the crowd cheers louder than ever before

"No citizen of my country should ever see suffering again! My bloodline will ensure it so! I will ensure it so!" He jumps from the roof of the truck as the crowd still cheering gathers thick around us, above the lightning clouds dissipate with a few light cracks of thunder following behind.

"Go to Ali my son, for now I must go!" He yells at me through the roaring applause of the crowd. Before I can agree or question, again I am blinded, followed by a thunderous roar that seemed to fade upward.

The crowd began to part so I decided to continue over towards the waiting Ali and Abigail, dining in a nearby deli. With the masses thinning out I could see the name of the business. Woodard's Deli and Meats. Written in dark purple with weird lettering on a dark tan backdrop. Inside I find them in a back corner both, Abigail enjoys a Banana Foster as Ali enjoys a pan seared lamb chop.

"They have desserts here too?" I ask as I approach the two, taking a seat near Abigail who as her back to the door.

"Oh, Ellis will make you anything, only us though." Abigail says as she cuts into what's left of her banana.

"Some speech huh?" Ali jokes lightning as she cuts into her chop, only partially eaten so far.

"He does that often?" Address the people? Put on fireworks?" I ask now browsing the menu.

"Oh yeah. It keeps up morale. Builds report." She replies taking a sip of what I could only assume is iced tea. Next thing I know the waiter approaches the table, I look up from the menu to see the same man from earlier, the brown-shirted man with the star of David.

"Hey, you were out there helping that couple." I say immediately without thinking too much into it.

"My sister and her fiancée sir, but yes that was I." He replies lightly shaking, rinsing his hands nervously in a large white cloth. He looks around the table, asking the girls if they want anything else, they nod to imply their satisfaction.

"That was awfully brave of you my good man, I get that that was family now but still, a lot of people back home would've just watched their blood get executed without saying a word." I say handing him the menu. "I'll take the pulled pork." I add as she takes the menu, stuffing it into his waistband, luckily, he had changed shirts to one less covered in blood.

"And where are you from, if I might ask." He responds happily put his hands on his hips aggressively.

"New York." I respond.

"That wild, me and my sister spent some time in New York too, originally we hail from Morocco but you know how it goes."

"What brought you here?" I ask before taking a sip of Abigail's water.

"Well we went to France first after Morocco, that's where my sister met her husband. God rest his soul. From there New York, New Orleans, Panama, then finally here. One thing I can say is I've never met anybody willing to let their family die if they aint got to." He finishes with a light smirk of joy preparing to get back to the kitchen.

"Wait, before you go, how's your sister?" I curiously ask with my knee on the red booth leather.

"The medics are taking her down at to St. Corinthians. She'll be okay, Sunlatveria has some pretty fancy hospitals." He sighs a sigh of relief and exhaustion.

"Don't you worry about her, I'll be headed out once I put your order in, 'Vante will bring you your food. Thanks again for all your family has done for us by the way. I'll get that order in right away." He turns again to head back into the kitchen through a large black and silver door.

"Ellis, right?" I yell, both knees now pinned into the leather. "I'm Harold, you can call me Harry." He pauses in the threshold turning to me.

"Nice to meet you Harold." He smiles before heading back into the kitchen.

"Making new friends 101." Abigail laughs as she finishes off her ice cream, I turn back into the seat, taking another helping of Abigail's iced water.

"Fancy hospitals?" I ask adjusting my shirt as Abigail continues to munch on her food.

"Few years back, your father convinced a group of scientists; Tesla, Einstein, Curie, some others whose names I cannot remember at the moment, to pay the island a visit, and by island of course I refer to the lake." Ali expels as she eats unmanneredly. "They helped him engineer some revolutionary stuff using the lake. Most of it was life changing medical stuff, utilizing the regenerative properties of the island, making the research useless anywhere outside Sunlatveria. Nikola helped bring free power to the entire island as well, which aided greatly in balancing the rapid increase of immigrants that were pouring in."

"Did he pay them? Trade some of the lakes water? How did he persuade them to come to the edge of the world and jump in a pool with him?" I needle further as the replacement waiter comes along with my plate.

"He didn't give them anything and he didn't have to convince them." Pointing her fork towards me as she looks up from the plate. "The stupefying properties of the lake, is enough, the chance to study something so miraculous, the chance to gaze upon god. How could they refuse?" She shrugs her shoulders looking back towards the platter of scraps. "For your information, there's another way into that chamber that doesn't include the vertigo pit, you'll find it eventually though." My eyebrows raise in amusement and absorption.

"For now, back to business." Ali says setting down her fork and knife. "While Edwin is gone, it falls to me to commence your tutelage."

"My training?" I ask contorting my face.

"First, we are to head over to the University in Thesis, a Professor Moton awaits to help you enroll so you can continue with your education." She cleans her face with the crumbled napkin cloth.

"Alright, I'm up for that, I've been thinking about finishing my engineering degree. What else, that's not really considered training."

"Well Edwin has already selected a line of courses for you, this way you'll be better suited to take over as once the time comes, but aside from that, I'll be overseeing your physical training each morning with some very impressive fighters from all around the globe, Edwin brought them here to train me." Shocked and disgusted I take a moment to look out of the window over to Cobain Square, the impact spot still lighting smoking.

"Ali is really good Harry, she taught Louise and Louise has been showing me some cool moves that you'd really get a kick out of, literally." Abigail speaks up finishing off her banana.

"That's insane I'm not going back to school if he's going to pick and choose every moment in my life going forward. I'm not going to be his puppet like Louise. If he expects me to perform, I will, but the road there will be travelled on my own terms." I exclaim before again turning back to the window, to the smoldering spot.

"Harold, think longtime, Louise is no puppet, she's the one who set us on the path to becoming the social paradise Sunlatveria is destined to be. Besides, Edwin's done this same thing with Louise, me and Abigail who's been in school for five months now. It's for the best, it's for the future and longevity of his dynasty and our land." Ali tries to plea with me to serve my father willfully and blindly.

"No, Ali, first it isn't the same for you. You're... immortal." I try to whisper the word. "Plus, you're in love with him, you're not family." I strop, crossing my arms leaning back and gain peering towards the charred crater as faceless hordes of citizens travel back and forth across my view. Despite not looking over at her, the silence told me everything. I'd hurt her, something I didn't mean to do.

"Look, how about this, I'll go down to the school tomorrow, enroll myself, but I'm going to need two electives all my own to choose, and the training has to be done by you and you alone." I turn to her, reaching my hand across the table awaiting a confirmation.

"Well... I don't know if Edwin would agree..." She wipes her hands with the napkin before grabbing mine softly, squeezing gently as we shake. "...But I think we can keep this between us." She smiles and again I find myself stuck for a moment, I can only smile back, trapped in her aweing beauty.

"Between us, right Abi?" I look down at her as we part hands.

"Of course, Harry, my lips are sealed!" She exclaims waving her fork high into the air, flinging ice cream as she went, a big glob hits Ali of her high right below her left eye. "Oops, I'm sorry Ali I didn't mean to."

"It's alright sweetheart." Ali laughs picking up her already used napkin.

"Hold on, let me get it." I pick up a fresh napkin from under my place setting and reach across the table. Ali smiling hard as she sat still, her head extended out towards me. I trembled lightly, almost too nervous to get this done in a smooth matter but I do, wiping away the cream before it has a chance to drip further down her gorgeous face and soon I am back with my hands at my side and for a moment we sit in an awkward silence.

I look back across the square to the smoldering spot, light speckles of blood had almost dried in the sun and were barely visible. A large blob of pedestrians pushes past, my eyes still locked on where the crater sat. Once a gap finally formed in the traffic, I couldn't believe what my eyes were telling me. The spot was gone, no smoldering ash, no dried-up blood, no broken pavement. It was fixed in a quarter of a second.

Without informing the girls, I vaulted over the booth seat backing as fast as I could, almost falling several times as I bolted out of the diner and across the street. I push and force my way through the horde, finally coming to spot I was sure laid the crater. Nothing out of the ordinary, the pavement was as it was before, perfect, clean, evenly cemented. It made no sense and in reaction I dropped to my knees, blankly staring at the slab when I feel a hand fall on my left shoulder.

"Impressive yes?" Ali says as she kneels next to me. "Look I can't explain it as well as others but simply but, the island has some sort of healing factor due to the lake. Like my own abilities, just on a larger scale." I take a sigh of relief before standing up.

"I'm just relieved I'm not delusional, I was certain I'd slipped into a psychotic episode." I joke as Abi emerges through the crowd from the diner.

"Nah, you're good, just too much fun for one day, come on lets head back to Solitude." Ali grabs Abigail by the hand and hooks her other around my arm as we begin walking towards the street to catch a taxicab.

"Wait, so what about the men?" I ask as around us the marketplace bustles once more.

"Oh, yes, they're dead, don't ask about those sea urchins again please." Ali responds laughing, the laughs cuts short to indicate that she was in fact serious about the matter.

I laugh as we stroll carelessly towards a waiting cab, my mind still kind of stuck on the tragedy that I'd just witnessed. I'd kept a straight face, as best as I could, through the entirety of the incident. It escapes me how Edwin, as smart he claims to be, could think public execution is the best strategy in winning over a people. The trident of raining lightning flashes in my head like a blaring horrendous reminder. I can understand they were ignorant xenophobes, but they were humans no less, who deserved trial, who deserved counsel, aid, they could have been mentally sick and he could've fixed them at the flick of his wrist. But instead he chose death, he himself, without any advising or due process, he chose as god would. Death, instant death, complete obliteration. Hell, if they had any family there would nothing to bury, not even a hunk of roasted leg.

I think back to six months ago when I first arrived, he made a German battalion turn around with their heads between their asses, he killed one guy that day and made a huge display of power before the crew hopped back onto their U-boat. This was different, there were no uniforms, no orders, just every citizen of New Shang to behold the atrocious act in person.

New Shang, one of the biggest port cities in the Southern Hemisphere right now, oh how tales of his tremendousness would spread through across the oceans. Some would hear it as legend, others challenge. My thoughts ran and ran as the taxi driver heads towards Solitude, and I find myself dozing off just as we exit New Shang, staring barrenly out the window at the passing landscapes with Abigail tightly wrapped my arm, coddled up against me already asleep from the ride so far.

"She's exhausted." Ali whispers low, her arm draped across the top of the seat, lightly she runs her hands through Abigail's hair.

"Long day." She adds, imperceptibly her hand moves from the entanglements of Abigail's hair as she drops over onto my lap. Her rough and sudden adjustments continued as she stretched her feet across Ali's lap, pressing her hands together under her head for support as she continued to sleep peacefully using us as a makeshift mattress.

We both smile making eye contact that last for a few seconds before we both turn back towards the window and the passing pastels. I feel her hand on my arm and in moments Ali is clinched around my arm with her head on my shoulder. She entangles her fingers with mine we both get comfortable for the long drove home. The cab turns onto the Jade highway; a twelve mile stretch of road that parallels the Jade river in both directions, splitting off around New Shang Bay and wrapping around Solitude Lake, I hear some locals refer to it as Highway 88 because of its loop.

I begin to drift off again as I settle my head back shutting my eyes. Alis head on my shoulder, Abigail laid across us, with the smoldering spot still parading through my mind like artillery fire in the night.

……………………………………………………………………………………………

I awake in an empty grey classroom, standing in the middle of what can only be described as the aftermath of a disaster. The tiling is a familiar dirty teeth kind of yellow, the beige and broken tables scattered about all around the clearing where I stood. Dropped in the middle of a bombed-out school, chalkboard broken in two on the floor, I anxiously examine my hands and my clothing when the creaking wooden door slams open with a loud thud as it bangs against the wall. An ethically ambiguous woman stands comfortably in the threshold enveloped in bright lights emitting from just outside the door. Nonchalantly she stood, swaddled in dull grey and black school attire leaning against the door pane with a handful of textbooks clutched into her chest.

"Delores?" I ask dumbfoundedly, reaching towards her like a lunatic pleading his sanity.

She speaks but her voice is mangled, inaudible despite seeing her perfect lips move around the various o's and a's. I try to move towards her but I soon realize as I reach and stumble forward that I haven't moved an inch. Still I stand in the center of the disastrous classroom, she waves for me to follow, still talking on not aware I can't hear a word. She flashes a giant smile at me, her cheeks shooting up as her eyes thin, she mouths a few more syllables I can't make out as the light from the hall shines in my face, before turning into the extremely lit hallway.

I scream and claw at nothing, facing the door, glued in my position, angrily I shout for her to come back. Viciously I struggle to move, pushing my leg forward as hard as I knew how as something began to happen around me. The room began to move, the walls spacing out about 40 meters each in a swift blink of the eye, the ceiling rose another 40 or 50 meters when water burst from one of the ceiling tiles and began flooding the room.

I'd realized this was dream, yet still I found myself stuck, unable to press forward no matter how much of myself I put into it. I began calling out my mother's name, my anger subsided and replaced with fear as I screamed for someone to wake me up. Soon I begin to yell for my father, helpless as the water rises above my chest.

"Stop this!" I yell as I continue to struggle towards the safety just beyond the mystic threshold. In the midst of this external struggle, an odd feeling in my stomach overtakes my attention. The warm squirming almost makes my gag when I try to picture what could be inside me, but before I have the chance to react, it shoots upwards out of my mouth splashing into the flooding room heavily.

The weird entity was no worm of flesh, but a worm made completely of light, the small foot long, two-inch-thick creature dropped into the rising mud colored water, writhing vigorously as it sank. Its shining essence shimmer brighter and a spiral of white electricity began to spin underneath. I wiped my mouth, taking a moment to examine the strange fluid leaking that the insect-like creature left on my lower lip. The same sparkling liquid energy from my father's dungeon.

The typhoon begins to pick up and the water began to whip furiously, again I attempt to move towards the door, not expecting a response as all the previous tries, but finally I move. I look up at the door that looks an inch closer and I begin to kick and wade my way through the spinning wave pool towards what I assumed was safety. I make it to the threshold of the door and suddenly the water stops. I get to my feet before turning into the class to see it in its best condition. The water completely gone, the hole in the ceiling repaired as if it never happened, the tables all upright in their correct position, the chalkboard fixed and in its place and covered with various Algebra equations.

Sighing I turn back out of the room towards the brightly lit hall when a massive beast, barely able to fit inside the hallway, slams fully into the doorway from the other side.

....

I'm sleep for what seems to be seconds before I am awaken by a loud crash against the side of the car. The impact flips us over a few times, flinging the driver form the front window in the process until we find ourselves finally stopped, propped up against a large tree about a hundred yards from the road. When I snap to from the initial shock, I make sure Abigail is alright, checking for anything broken or bleeding, when I spot Ali climbing her way out of the top of the overturned vehicle.

"Ali, wait!" I yell before she's gone out of view. Abigail tugs my shirt and begins to crawl around the seats towards the bloodied and shattered front windshield. Just then we both freeze when we hear a loud roar nearby, the strange roar had never been heard by either of us, low yet shrilling, thunderous yet eerie.

"What is that Harold?" Abigail ask quietly shaking.

"Hold on." I whisper as I slowly remove my jacket, gently spreading it over the next section of loose flesh and broken glass. I motion for her to follow me as I take the lead moving out of the now smoking vehicle. From crawling to crouching we make our way around the back of the large oak tree find a vantage point behind some bushes near the accident when we hear another, shorter roar followed by thundering footsteps.

"Where's Ali?" Abigail whispers crouching behind me as I peer over an odd freshly cut tree stump that contained light buzzing swirls of blue and white laced within the wood. I scan the area looking for Ali's dress and when I finally spot her I freeze in silence with Abi still tugging on my shirt for answers. Ali, only a few centimeters shorter than myself, stood in front of a massive leering jet black beast with the body of a bulldog, trailing behind it sported a large brown colored beaver tail. Ali stood fearlessly with her hand extended upward, towards its twisted face that resembled a boar, assumingly attempting to calm the monstrous hybrid.

A beam of sunlight peers through the treetop canopy, reflecting off a piece of metal just behind the animal. I see the driver, his legs mangled by the mysterious hybrid, his face bloody and scrapped from the crash. He'd somehow managed to pull a gun from his inner coat, aiming it at the behemoths back. Frightened, he fires every bullet in the clip leaning up against another giant tree and the noise alone sends a shiver up the monsters' spine causing him to buck back roaring loudly. One of the wild kicks hits the suffering driver, smashing his head in against in the tree.

I look over at Ali who still stands in idle fortitude, the tattoos running up and down her arms and legs glowing lightly now, the same light blue and white buzz of the tree stump I cower behind in awe. Ali begins to jog lightly at the raging beats now beginning to stampede towards her.

"ALI!!!" Me and Abigail both scream in terror as Ali jumps up one of the monsters' badger like arm like a spider leaping from one branch to the next. With a final powerful push, she leaps high into the air over the monsters' head, her tattoos glowing heavier than ever as a small dagger made of light manifests in her hand. Like a falling pigeon feather, she lands just in the middle of its brow, the blade now much longer than before as it pierces through the demon's skull and emerges from the bottom of his jaw. With another push, she backflips from the monsters flailing body as it falls to the ground, scrapping along another few feet before finally coming to a complete stop, blood splattering and drenching the dirt and the once radiant grass. Ali's last flip lands her just a few yards in front of where Abi and I watch waiting.

"That. Was. Amazing!!!" Abigail screams as she shoots through the pushes hugging Ali tightly. A line of blood sits already stale diagonally across her beautiful face.

"Incredible, right? Come on you too." She reaches and pulls me from behind the stump, pushing us all towards the road and away from the scene draping her arms across our shoulders, her tattoos back to solid black as before.

"What, was that?" I ask curiously still panicked, I had a thousand questions and I had to start somewhere, besides this was the first I'd heard or seen of Ali possessing any strange power, any specialty at all besides her slow aging.

"Yes, please tell me the story behind that knife you pulled." Abigail adds as we make it to the ditch aside the road, kicking some debris as I assist Abigails' climb up the steep.

"Well what do you guys want to know first? I mean, what don't you already know? Harold you've been here for over six months now, Abi I understand she's only been here a month now but you, what have you been doing with your time? You haven't started training yet, and from what I hear from your mother, when she's not side-eying me of course, is that you basically dropped out of school to come here." Ali expels as we embark down the road, the sun lowered now in the West bringing the sky to a gorgeous twilight of fading colors and light, stars twinkled to the East over the mountains. A warm breeze bushes between us as we walk shoulder to shoulder with Ali in the middle, her now dinghy dress lightly pattered with loose animal fur.

"Start with the beast." I say, scanning the passing tree line for movements.

"Alright, well that particular beast is cataloged in your father's records as a Badgerboar, but my people called the creatures the Oodem. They are by-products of the lake if I'm right, I'd thought we had hunted them into extinction, but I guess not."

"By-products?" Abi scratches her head.

"That group of scientists I mentioned earlier Harold? They helped Edwin map out a series of underground streams, tunnels and rivers that run beneath the island and more."

"And more?" I ask as she pauses, we approach an intersection, no vehicles or carriages had gone by, I was hoping for one here so we waited a moment.

"Well the underground web extends southwest beyond the coast, under the Pale Sea. I don't think Edwin has explored it yet but a few entrance ways have been uncovered. My entire life there has only been this island, but he suggests a larger continent once lied just south west of the Theos Mountain range that cups our southern coast."

"Yeah, I read his journals from his arrivals, he believes this island is just the tip of a continent larger than South America, just sunken underwater." I add leaning up against the traffic sign as Abi takes a seat on a convenient bench facing the road under the light post.

"Not sunken, destroyed, by the great lightning bolt that decimated my ancestors' civilization. Somehow my tribe survived, the land here was already special before the strike. Years past, generations came and went. Finally, I found myself alone, see I was royalty at one point."

"You're basically still royalty." Abi snickers as Ali takes a seat next to her brushing her hair with hands laughing.

"Yeah but to a different people, my own people. Anyway, I was born in the lake, one of the first in generations. My people would die soon after." Ali stops ruffling Abi's hair and turns towards the trees across the road, still no one had come by.

"What's become of the tunnel network?" I say trying to get her back on point and away from her own thoughts.

"Right." She snaps back to me. "The lake is the hub, for about 97% of that network."

"So that's how the island heals itself, how its kept itself safe all these millennia since the event. The energy being distributed into every corner, seeping into every lifeform. That must be how that Tesla guy managed to engineer that free energy solution so quickly, the power was already there." My minds racing, finally piecing together my Edwin clung to this land so valiantly and why Ali and Louise idolized him so. He was their protector.

"Edwin saw the lake and used it in a way no one had ever used it before. My people wasted its potential, using it to farm and for medicine. My birth was against the tribe councils' orders, yet here I am. He wants to share that power with you Harold. He sees a destiny for you, for all of us here." She looks up at me from the bench, hands clasped together in her lap, anxiously my eyes shoot to the small area of sidewalk that had been cemented just for this bench and streetlight.

I hear a rustle in across the street in the bushes, when I turn I spot a derby hatted gentleman appearing from the tree line on the opposite un-lit corner. The man spots our trio and struts gallantly across the pavement, sporting a thick brown handlebar mustache and donned in a black and white suit that was much too gaudy for the common immigrants that island had drawn in. As he comes closer, my focus shifts to his walking stick. I can out a double-barreled shotgun in his hand being used some sort of cane/crutch/deadly firearm abomination. Despite the oddness of the concoction, it was lined in pristine wood paneling with dark gold trimming.

"My lord, is that the brightest star I've seen in my life or am I going blind!?" He speaks up as he hits the curbs, grabbing the girls' attention suddenly motioning towards Ali for a hug. His accent a heavy British English, yet soothing and light despite the English accent stereotypes, a tongue very much matching his gentleman clothing.

"Professor Clarke! What a surprise, how nice to see you." Ali stand to hug the man with a widening smile on her face. "What are you doing so far from the university?" She adds with a look of relief and admiration brightening across her face. She gasps suddenly, covering her mouth with her wrist. "The Oodem."

"Exactly right my former student." He nods his cane towards her before removing his hat to introduce himself to Abigail and I. "Excuse me for my manners." He glances to Abigail first, bowing very formally, looking up at her.

"Professor Thornwood Leonardo Clarke, and suppose this is the lovely Abigail? Curious and brave younger sibling to..." He stands straight and turns to me, extending his right hand towards my waist. "Harold Hebrank. The demigod and heir to be. How are you my kin?" I push up off the light post and complete his handshake, smiling lightly.

"Kin?" I ask puzzled, his handshake is firm and lasting.

"We are all children of the Earth Harold." His pullback is genuine and kind, his overall aura one of sturdy foundation.

"Alright." I can't muster up a response and pause speechless in the brittle moment of one's first impression. He stares back into my soul for a bit before letting out a light laugh, forcing him to coddle his side.

"The badgerboar Ali, so you've seen it?" He says adjusting his self as he turns towards Ali.

"Yes professor, it demolished a taxi that was carrying us back to Solitude. The wreckage is about one hundred and fifty meters up this road." She motions up the dark path we'd walked from, even darker than the last time I'd checked.

"Well the three of you look just about..." He leans back to quickly examine Abi and I one more time. "...fairly alright. So, I assume you murdered the poor beast, is, that right?" He finishes places his hat back on before taking a seat on the bench next to Abi where Ali once sat.

"Poor beast? I may not be from here but I that that statement is crazy sir." I shout, upset that he would defend the monster that almost took my sisters life.

"Relax Harold, on top of teaching world history and biology at the university, he's also sits on the SPB, or the Sunlatverian Preservation Board." She interjects calming me down.

"Quite right Ali, and Harold I really think it's about time you wandered your way into one of my classes, from what I hear from your father your current lifestyle is not to his liking." I scoff loudly as I cross my arms.

"Edwin seems to discuss my future with every figure in Sunlatveria but refuses to drop the act and be a father or a husband."

"Man will be man, you will learn. The badgerboar, we'd thought they were wiped out in the hunting raids on '22. Three straight months, Edwin, I and a host of others charted every square inch of the islands surface, most of the more savage wildlife that used to roam the island were sent barreling into extinction.

"Seems you boys missed a few." Abigail comments cleverly, looking over at me smiling.

“We missed quite a few, some of the creatures are smart, very tricky to pin down. It was two years ago that the SPB was founded, after a family of farmers was found massacred outside Volstagg. The SPB was brought about for a multitude of preservation concerns, but the most relevant being to track these creatures classified as savage and quarantine their wandering grounds if possible.”

“What killed them?” Abigail spoke up.

“We could never identify the claw marks or the footprints, perhaps a monster we’ve yet to come across.”

“If possible?” I ask, leaning back against the post.

“Ali? What happened with the beast.” He turns his head up at her, ignoring my inquisition.

“I tried to pacify it, if I had more time I would have. The taxi driver, he was badly hurt from the initial crash, he had a firearm, he must’ve though…” Clarke raises his hand to stop her.

“Enough. I understand, you can’t control the actions or interpretations of others.” He sighs heavily, I was unsure if it was from relief or just grief.

“A shame, like I said before. But to answer your question from before Harold, often these animals are so barbaric in the mid that attack is their only response to opposing life. Thus, my blunderbuss here, unfortunate it’s been used more than I'd it to." He lays flat the cane across his lap as he sits back against the bench.

"How can you feel guilt..." Again, I interject. "...what about those raids you mentioned over a decade ago. You, my father, men stomped across this *beautiful* island and brutally murdered every *opposing* life you could find, hybrid hell-spawn or not.

"What would you have done child? The council voted to relocate them to a tight zoo in New Shang. Other voted to sell the meat at profit in South American and South Asia. We did what did thought was best, for the islands wildlife as well as the growing population. We reduced to wildlife population to a single percentage, preventing further harm to the islands citizens. We seek now to preserve the life of all creatures; every day we strive to undo the damage we've done in our most early days of infancy."

Bright lights peer over the hill coming from the direction of Shang, I make out that it's another black taxi as in gets closer.

"Perfect." I say as I motion the girls to get ready. The vehicle slows to a stop and the driver rolls down the passenger window, Ali flashes a card and the driver nods his head.

"Well I guess this is goodbye my dear Ali, please do come by the office tomorrow, bring Harold if he allows." He whispers as he and Ali hug.

"Of course, Professor, do you wish to ride with us? It's awfully late." She pauses at the door as Abigail hops into the back of the cab.

"No thanks my dear, that badgerboar was part of a large family that I intend to find by weeks end." She kisses him on the cheek before hopping into the back of the cab as well. Me and Clarke shake hands before departing and in no time, Ali lets her head fall to my shoulder, Abigail again stretches herself across our laps in a futile attempt to find sleep. After a few minutes of watching the darkness roll pass, I glance to the girls, both sleeping as the cab rumbles through the silent forest.

Chapter 2

Signs in The Sun

Six Years Later

I'd always been by my father's side since before he found his paradise. I was his little Lulu. It didn't matter to him that I wasn't his biological daughter, he's always treated me like the center of his world. Once we found we the island, of course his protective nature only increased a hundred-fold. I think back often on those first days, I was still at a young age yet he had me steering droves of men as they plowed fields and set foundations. Edwins' power could only go so far in aiding the development of a young nation, but that power was rivaled by the bracing tenacity of his thinking and will.

Father had always been the most intelligent being on the island, for a while in my teenage years I was sure his mental capacity dwarfed everyone on Earth. That was until he started the Beyonders Party. He assembled some of the smartest minds from around the globe, luring them with promises of land, power, freedom. Science was a very controversial topic in the outer world, here he promised there would be no eyes over their shoulders, no hands in their pockets, no lesser minds in their studies. Promises of moral neutrality brought scores of scientists from every corner of the world. Researchers and inventors seeking refuge from war and prying government, could find haven, just as the workers did running from taxation and debt.

We would have no bank from which a tax could be collected, no military to colonize and advance. We would be like the first settlers of Mu, working for the betterment of each other instead of written law or even the faux laws presented by countless faiths around the world. We would be the shining examples of humanity, the Beyonders. Father even let me attend several meetings, introducing me to many iconic figures at the time. Together they helped shoot Sunlatveria into full-blown super power status in a fraction of the time when compared to normal human advancement.

The group is even responsible for the Vizanti council, after so many invasions attempts, the council was created to represent the major powers of the political world, the hold their militaries at bay while feeding them all false information regarding the island and their other allies abroad. Before long the Beyonders disbanded amidst the confusion of the first world war, retreating either to their home countries or retiring along Sunlatverias southern coast. The council grew stronger without the cabal of scientist to keep them in check, despite their arrogance Edwin always managed to keep them in check. Besides his immense power, he was a skilled negotiator and was always very intimidating. His clothing always dark, after a while he was never seen without his signature dark plated armor and cape. He became a symbol to the masses that has washed ashore seeking forgiveness and solace.

Churches would spring up in his honor and overnight he would disband them. Zipping across the skies of the city like a god, he never used violence on the island. It was always talking, debating, calming people down or making them understand why what they were doing was wrong. We didn't need a police force, a military, a power plant, nothing. I've seen multiple navies, waving multiple flags pass through, lightning strikes the beaches and they leave. He'd really only murdered a handful of people in the twenty years before Harold appeared, but of course day one of Harold being on the island I get a report about a German sub landing near Theseus. I'd hoped father was beyond killing, but I assume he had to make a spectacle for his newly discovered *son*.

It's been over six years since Harold first appeared in our lives. At first I couldn't stand the little bugger, father talked him up about him being in school and working and to provide for Abigail and his mother but from what I've seen, from the moment he stepped foot on the island he's been a lazy, no good, unambitious sight-seer. Upon asking him now he'd say side-step the observation, calling it an insult from his big sister trying to show dominance. Perhaps he felt cheated, out of a lavish island dreamscape and was instead forced to feed from the gutter of New York. I should have a sit down with him one of these to get his true feelings out about me, he's always so distant from the family just like Edwin.

At least I can understand Edwin, he's fighting the war from a hundred angles, whilst since continuing to run his home nation effectively and confidently. But through all Harolds schooling, training, and teaching, he lives here, and still should be able to make time for the family. Mal I know spends most of her time in the garden with Abi, Abigail who's also heavily involved in school and training, the young girls heart still directs her home every night. Today was Harold's birthday and one of the only common interests we have is automobiles, so I bought him a welcoming surprise, had to get it shipped all the way from Nevada but I know he's just going to love it.

"Louise?" A knock is heard to the door behind me where I sit at the all-white and wicker vanity mirror. It was Ms. White, my head handmaiden since I was fourteen, she was an immigrant from Haiti, a teacher and a nanny back home. At the time my father was interviewing every single person that landed on the beach, after a while it got too much, luckily, he found her before he ceased the strenuous work.

"I'm almost ready Barb, just finishing my hair." I turned back around to tie my hair up with a dark blue band to match my blouse, hat and shoes.

"Well the car is here to take you the Oceanology Society." Barbara White says peering at the back of my head as I continue messing with my hair responding with a light sigh.

“In my opinion my lady, you shouldn’t be wasting your precious time on these pitiful social gatherings. You need to be on zeppelin or fancy yacht traveling the world while you’re still so young. You’ve been so preoccupied with the refugees, you’ve haven’t taken time for yourself in months.” Barb tries to joke about the current state of my failing career while all the same insulting me. I turn around towards her scoffing as I throw my hands down into fists.

“Now Miss White, you know very while they island is my home and there is nowhere else in the world I’d rather be. I’ve seen everything I’ve needed to see. I have evidence in the form of the countless nights spent digging my way out of the pile of books provided by my father. You should know better than anybody, I see this land as the highest, nothing beyond the oceans can rival or compare. Traveling? What a wash, the people of the world? Barbaric.” I can feel how thick I’ve filled the room with tension, my hair in a fluster again from the heavy movements that erupted, luckily this is Miss White, a someone who has seen worse of me.

“My dear.” She approaches with a sincerity on her face, a light smile as she caresses my arm. “I hear you Lou.” A method she’s used since she’s been with us, instantly covering the flames. I close my eyes and take a few breathes. “A little on edge this morning?” She fixes my hair before taking a seat near the door.

“It’s the ground breaking of the new Science Center off Belmont in Volstagg. Someone from the family needs to be there to represent our name. I don't understand what's been going on with father but lately he's just... off."

"Off, my lady? And what of young Harold, I don't see much of him around Solitude these days."

"Yes, well I guess the concern with father dates to when he back from Poland last November. See my father, when he flies to certain locations in the atmosphere, can hear almost every radio and broadcast signal in the world. I'm not sure about the specifics of his power but I know he's come to me with vast caches of knowledge and stories that would bewilder me for days. One night, he always preferred to travel at night, while up there floating peacefully in the clouds he heard a broadcast that made him react without thinking. That broadcasts origin was Germany, Nazi commanded Berlin, Germany. Hitler and his Third Reich were committing atrocities across the entire spectrum of the fascist party's rise to power."

Walking side by side through the innards of the castle, we make our way towards the driveway and the waiting car, all the while I talk, Miss White follows observantly, apparently never have heard the stories of my father before.

"I've heard many scary things about what those Nazis are up, tell me please, what did your father hear?" She asks so enthusiastically that I almost feel compelled to spill more of my father's secrets than I already had.

"Whatever he heard Miss White, he zipped straight to the origin point. I don't know what he saw, what he heard, or what the bloody hell happened over there. But I do know this, he caught a stray bullet in the back on the head." We step through the final threshold onto the sunbaked driveway, the car about ten yards away with the driver already standing by the door, hands crossed.

"But how!? I figured he was invincible. How did he make it home? Let alone survive?!" Miss White scratches her head in amazement and confusion.

"Don't worry Miss White." I smile laughing as we linger by the house for a minute. "I have to go alright, we can finish talking later."

"Oh yes, I do want to hear the end of this tale. Have a lovely day my dear, don't let those stuffed shirted bastards ruin this lovely weather." She waves me away as I hop into the car, the driver introduces himself as if he hasn't driven me before. Franco. He must think I'm the type of royalty that can't tell their staff apart.

My mind goes back to my father in Poland as he begins the drive, I stare intensely out the window, admiring the beautifully colored and vibrant landscape.

Somehow my father lowered his guard, for some reason his put down his shield and somehow managed to get shot in the head. By the time he returned a week later, it was just a grisly scar just behind his right ear. But I knew, it wasn't there before, and on top of that it was one of the first times he'd returned exhausted. He'd been out throwing tanks and ripping apart whaling vessels, come home ready to take me to school, ready to take me here, there. But that was the first time he returned with a gloom, he returned as if he'd seen the very worse in mankind and was ready to throw them into the fire. The look on his face, he considered himself their judge, their jury, their prosecutor, all the while being their protector. But on this night, he no longer saw them, people, humans everywhere, as worth the effort.

The car begins the loop around the glorious Solitude Lake, the driver attentive at the wheel, quiet in his work as the local big band radio station plays on a lowered volume. My gaze returns to the exterior before he can catch my eyes examining him. The lake shining as always, so reflective one must shield his or her eyes when taking awe upon its beauty. Soon its immense sparkle disappeared behind a thicket of bush and vegetation, we were turning towards the farmlands outside Volstagg. My mind goes back to my father and how he'd be different. Not leaving the island, nor any public appearances. Forgetting simple stuff like dates, times, names, verses, scriptures. There's a plethora of information he has passed down to me that now he can't remember.

The biggest reveal of his decaying mental state comes from a much more personal stance. My father taught me how to play chess at a very young age. He was very skilled, I didn't manage my first win against the old man until I was three years into college and even that think a lot of study and strategic preplanning. But last week I obliged him into playing a game with me and all was fine at first. Twenty minutes in he starts to move a pawn as if it was a rook, I look up at him oddly but his face was unturned. Sure, he'd made the right move he went back to his bible, something he'd kept with him a lot since the second war had started.

He never released he made the mistake, I never said a thing, I proceeded to win as was the usual these days. But I could tell he'd lost more than his foresight. Besides his mental straining, his physical appearance was untouched, a blessing of the lake a stark contract against the curse of his failing genius, his dimming ambition and his darkening thought. And as hard as it is the embrace the possibility of life without him, I am forced to set aside my personal fear for the sake of the nation he'd built. Who would provide the light piercing through the darkness as he had for the last three decades?

As the car turns a final corner, the tall bright blue and pink building complex of the Oceanology Society comes into view just down the road. The drive is beautiful, the Society sits on a cliff just above a seaside village called Renku. The village only sports about four or five families. I can make out a few people lounging near the beach on all white docks and boathouses. Further In the water I see some swimmers out about hundred meters form the shore. I fear they get caught in the razor reef, the deadly underwater forest surrounds the island and at some its inner trees stretch inward as far as three hundred meters from land.

Just as we make our way to the top of the hill towards the Society building, through the thicket of trees to my right shines a bright familiar light flowed by loud roars of a dying whale.

“Did you hear that?” I ask to the driver. He turns back, one hand on the wheel.

“Hear what my lady?” As he finishes his reply, through the windshield I see a large reddish creature being thrown from the trees.

“WATCH OUT!” I scream for him to turn around but its too late, he whips the wheel to swerve but smacks directly into the monster. The car thuds over it heavily before screeching to a halt in the middle of the road.

“Was that a Scorpion-Moth?” I ask the driver after a quick sigh of relief. The windshield is covered in a thick shield of green and red insect gore. The driver doesn’t respond, his hands stuck to the steering wheel shaking.

“I’ll give you a minute Franco.” I step out of the car, shutting the door behind me as I see Ali and Harold stepping from the trees.

“Louise!” Ali runs over give me a hug. The glow of her tattoos fading, powering down. “I can always count on you.” Ali adds eyeing the dead bug smooshed on the road just behind the car.

"Hello Ali, Harold. What are you two doing down here this time of day?" I ask as I break from Ali, Harold approaches, crossing his arms as he hovers near Ali.

"Moth hunting, you know how the locals get when they see something that doesn't fit their worldly view. Even in paradise there must be something to disgust the individual." Ali replies snickering with a hand on her hip, looking over to Renku in the distance.

"Locals, family, what's the difference. And Harold how are doing on this fine day brother?" I ask looking him up and down. They both were covered in dirt and insect blood.

"Like she said, moth hunting. We stumbled across a nest, we hadn't planned on killing any to be honest but..."

"Once one got our scent, they all got out scent." Ali interrupts.

"It was a bloodbath sister." Harold says sighing trying to clean his shirt as he examines the animal under the car. "Ah shit, my Sabina is all bent up under your car."

"Yeah well." I add laughing. Behind me I hear Franco sped off in his car, apparently, he'd finally awaken from his trance and deciding it best to high tail it home.

"Guess your driver is new to the island." Harold laughs wrapping his filthy arm around my shoulder. I shrug it off without much thought.

"Never seen a giant scorpion-moth eh?!" Harold yells at the car as it fades in the distance towards the Society just over the hill. "Ah, what a block head. Where you headed anyway Lou" He finishes.

"Up the hill. The oceanology Society has a new center, I'm going for the groundbreaking."

"Hmm, that's odd, why aren't there more cars going up this road then?" He questions looking North down the long road we'd just come.

"If you must know brother I'm late, but that doesn't mean I can't still talk to members and socialize. They left a very important ribbon cutting for an exhibit untouched just for my arrival though." I add as I tie up my dress to begin walking.

"Lou, I think your car is coming back." Ali says still facing the incline. Me and Harold turn to see Franco, zooming crazily our way. He zips by us without bothering to stop or glance despite me waving my arms intensely and screaming profanities at him.

"Why didn't he stop?" Harold asks scratching his head as he watches Franco disappear around a bend.

"He's frightened." Ali says calm, still facing the hill.

"It was only a big bug, and he killed it for blasted sakes." Harold argues. "What could be here to fear, a good portion of the Hebrank clan is right here so why abandon the Despots daughter. He had only one simple task. Escort you up the hill. I'm sorry sis but am I wrong for being upset for you." Harold pleads to me with his nose growing red.

"Harold." Ali shuts him up with a world. We all focus on the hill and that when I hear the buzz. A low-pitched buzz, gradually increasing in range. My eyes widen, my stomach tightens and my heart starts to beat louder and louder, echoing within my chest. The realization hits me like bad opium.

"Bombers." I say it aloud and Harold turns his head to me as he silently readies his fighting stance. As his head turns back, a horde of white red Airplanes break over the Horizon of road and trees from the Southern coastline.

"Who are they!?" Ali yells over the roaring of over a hundred war machines bustling above.

"Japanese Air Force!" I yell back. "Come on, follow me." I exclaim as loud as I can as I begin a light sprint up the hill for a better view. The deafening swarm continue to press North without dropping a shell. We make it the curve of the hill, Loud bangs and explosions can be heard far away off coast and I can finally see the Oceanology Society building. All the members are outside curious of the noise, about thirty people all huddled along the edge of most southern facing cliff, fenced along with short wooden railing. Across the waters dotting the horizon, dozens of watercraft vehicles ranging from aircraft carriers to submarines.

Explosions rock across the waters in-between where the Japanese navy idled and the island itself.

"What are they doing?" Harold asks as we reach the cliff railing right next to the Society members.

"Destroying the reef." One member of the Society speaks up over the mummering group.

"If they break through they'll be able to land on the beaches!" Another one yells in panic.

"They sure didn't do their homework." I snarl for a second in the waning glimmer of hope if only by natural stalling.

"Luckily for us, they picked the thickest spot of the reef." Ali adds from behind.

"Do you think the reef will manage? How long do we have?" Harold presses.

"The rate in between how fast their artillery can destroy the razor forest is rivaled by the speed at which the island heals itself. We have much more pressing matters on our hand Harold. You need to focus on the task at hand. Ali, can you get to Edwin in-time?" Looking back at her staring upward at the whizzing airplanes.

"He should be in his study this time of day, right?" She replies finally looking down, her face lightly phased by the invasion.

"Of course." She replies checking her pocket-watch as quickly as she can. "Those bombers look like they are heading to New-Shang. I say you've got about fifteen to eighteen minutes."

"That means I have time." Without thought she crouches quickly before gracefully leaping impossibly high into the air.

"Take out as many as you can along the way!" I yell as she soars away, blue and white streaks of electricity and light appearing behind her as she catches on to the wing of one of the bombers. Immediately it picks up smoke, falling out of the aerial formation, descending over the distance towards Solitude Lake as she leaps from the wreckage towards another awaiting bomber.

"Can you do that?" I ask him speedily. As the swarm finally passes overhead.

"Umm well she was practically born and raised in the lake, I've yet to even stick a toe in.. Father has tried to... baptize me but I refused, the ceremony he proposed was too theatrical, too gloomy for me." He gives me a look of confusion.

"So how have you been out fighting Scorpion-moths?"

"Ali has been sneaking out crystal shards charged with the lakes energy, power gets transferred through a quick injection in the arm, last a good hour if I'm lucky.

Were beyond that threshold." He lowers in head in disappointment.

"Well shit you're a useless druggie just like dad. God dammit, we need to find a way to stop this." I say exhausted from the random chaos of the day that was meant to be so meaningless. There is a moment of silence, Harold drops him arms to his sides still facing the red-eyed fleet abroad. I grip the railing facing the same way, my grip tightens and begins stripping the wood, blood trickles down my right-hand dripping into the dirt from the splinters. This is my home, I won't stand by and let them destroy it. I cant.

"What of us dear lady?" Says one of Society members, effetely shutting the groups disorder down. I wipe my face and eyes before turning around, sure my nose was now apple red.

"Right, all of you, in your cars and to your homes immediately." Without though they begin a frenzy to their cars and down the road. One of the Society approaches me before he departs, dressed in an all-black pin stripped suit. "No need for any of you to be out in harm's way when the hammer comes down, now is it?

"My lady, the exhibit that we wanted you to open. I think you'll find it helpful to you and yours." He whispers elegantly. "A secret gift from my family to yours." He tips his hats before starting a light strut down the road.

"Wait, who are you? Where's your car?" I'd spent time on all the scientific circles around the island, I'd never seen this man and I was sure I was at the point where I knew all interesting faces on the island.

"I walked here madam, and I am no one of interest." He turns again towards the road of fleeing vehicles and begins his walk. A light strut, he carried himself as if nothing that could possibly happen hear affect him. If it wasn't for his middle Eastern accent and dark skin, I'd be sure he was a spy.

"Come one Harold." I head into the Society behind, everything so brand new and freshly painted and opened.

"What are we to find in here to help?" Harold asks as he peers around the large main room, eyeing to various exhibits and pieces.

"Back here." I spot the uncut tape of an exhibit covered behind a red curtain with black lace. A little title sign on the front of the railing read "Just Out of Reach, at the bottom of this pool sits the entrance to an underground cave, once followed this cave is theorized to connect with a much large network of underground rivers and canyons that span the entirety of island. There is also a much larger network under the Southern sea that is still unexplored. Not much is known about what lies at the bottom of this network, or what creatures swim about. The Oceanology Society build this new center around this pool."

I dramatically pull the curtain down revealing a large pool of still dark water about four meters in diameter.

"What a lackluster place this is, can we leave." Harold sits down on the edge of the pool. I try to peer into the dark pool, not even a shimmer of light from the bottom. My heart again begins to race as I formulate a plan.

"At the bottom of this cave, sits your future brother."

"What do you mean?" He starts trying to see through the misty shadow sitting atop the pond.

"Fathers power, you've seen where it comes from yes? Well his private pool is only a piece of a much larger connected system underneath the island." I finish as he jumps from the ledge and starts to read the plague assigned to the pool.

"Hold on... Ali told me about this a long time ago. She said the island was basically a giant living entity and that Sunlatveria is only a fraction of the beast that lies beneath the ocean floor. She said the mythical streams are responsible for the flora and flora as well as the grab-bag of animals, insects and birds."

"Well, she's partially correct. But, you understand that in order to save the island, our home, you must swim to the very depths of this system and find the energy hidden below, yes?"

"Wait why am I doing this? You've been going on and on since I got here how you should be the boss instead of me. Hell, I believe you, I've seen you do more for the citizens here than any member of that council, hell even more that Edwin. All you need is an amazing powerset to match that amazing and brilliant mind of yours."

"Harold." I blush for a moment before the crushing weight of reality sets in after half a second.

"Is this about father? He'll show." He asks seriously.

"Harold." My serious tone returns. "This pool is over five hundred meters deep, and that's just recorded darkness. Who knows how much deeper you'll have to travel before you find what you need. This has nothing to do what how ever since he discovered you, it's all he's talked about, all he's wanted. You can see it on his face when he looks at you versus me, and it wasn't always like that. You taking his place, taking his name. You taking the power that he sees you as being the only one worthy enough for." I bow my head. "Besides, I've seen its power and I decline just like I've always declined. I may not agree with most of father's rhetoric, but I will follow his wishes. You've seen him lately yes?"

"Yes, I'm not sure I see what you mean. Yeah he's been forgetful but…"

"Are you going to jump into the damn pond or should I Harold! You're out fighting monsters in the woods, so surely you can hold your breath long enough to save my fucking homeland." I scream, frustrated with everything. In a moment its still, the bombings from the water still going on outside, only now getting closer.

"You have no faith in father?" He asks, again sitting on the edge removing his shoes and hiking up his pants.

"It will show you everything and answer all your questions, just trust in yourself." I distract him, helping him remove his blood lathered jacket. "Believe in yourself Harold, you can do this brother. All your hard work, ends here." I kiss him on the cheek before he dives in feet first. Soon I can no longer see him as he disappears beneath the smoggy water.

The bombardment continues are besides that all else is quiet as the waters again grow calm, only rippling with the shockwaves outside.

"Please Harry, you can do this." I'm not a good swimmer anyway. I've been terrified of underwater in general ever since we first landed here. I'm not looking for any excuses to go back in. Three minutes' pass and I grow worried. Soon, a light shines immensely from the depths of the pool and in seconds a streaks of lightning shoots upward, blasting from the pond and straight through the

Society buildings innards before bursting from the roof straight into the sky.

The sun was setting in the West, drawing a grey twilight over the island. I rush outside, scanning the horizon as best I could. Towards the fleet, I try to follow Harold with my eyes, he shoots like a falling comet towards the still firing fleet. From the cliff, I see him far off the coast near the militia, he stops midair, after floating idle for a moments, absorbing gunfire and direct shelling. I blink and in a split second he's chopping up the giant cruisers with enormous beams of brightly sparking light blue electricity. The sailors fire wildly at the infant god-king floating above them, maybe one of their shell gets lucky and manages a blessing from their god. Instead they panic like ants, scurrying into the water as the vessels sink slowly into the Nisha reef barrier. In large sweeps of his arms, Harold splits five or six ships at once. Melting straight through from port to starboard with the intensity of a hundred suns. His disintegrating gaze covered a thick area, each arm moving inductively on their own. His continuous beams of white and indigo seemed to vibrant and appear phantasmal as he vaporized the remaining invaders swimming about the wreckage and entropy.

Behind me I hear a bang. A bomb, an explosion of some sorts. But only one. There were hundreds of planes but there was only this one loud bang. Louder than any mortar or distillery accident or lightning strike I'd ever heard. It rings through my body, vibrating the space in-between my skin and my bones. Turning towards the inner island, taking my eyes of Harold of the coast busy with the

Japanese navy, I see the still resonating membrane of vast reaction of energy towards New Shang. A huge explosion still masses. The sun still setting just behind the blast unlike anything I'd ever seen, almost blotting out the sun setting just off in the background. Mixed throughout the spherical devastation ran dark red streaks of electricity, the colors faded as loose flares of purple and black lightning spark off in every direction.

"No... My people." Before I can drop to my knees, another streak of energy streaks overheard a few dozen meters. Harold. Headed towards the expanding bubble at speeds rivaling Edwin at his prime.

"Save us brother. Please."

Chapter 3

The Rivers Edge

While I’d only known my older sibling for a handful of years, I loved Louise. I knew she was using me, always manipulating me to further her different agendas. All noble causes though so I never complained much. Fighting father and the council, in public and private over civil rights, environmental protections, sometimes pushing as far a complete government overhaul. She was tough and wouldn't back down against a room full of old men in vest stuffed with ridiculous pocket squares.

She was right though, I had a dose of the lightning around noon when me and Ali first trekked out towards a tiny coastal village named Renku just outside Volstagg, Southeast of Solitude. They were being plagued by giant flying scorpions. These ugly monsters were feasting on the farmer's livestock in the night.

Ali would either sneak me into Edwins underground cavern for a quick drink or sneak me a random crystal shard that she'd dip into the magical pond. The latter involved me being stabbed unexpected by Ali, usually sneaking up behind me catching me off guard. The shook brings me to my knees every time. No matter how fast it heals after, or how the stabbing initially happens, the pain is immense, my joints lock as I fall and struggle to reach wherever she'd stab me today. The hell is worth it, always. Like one of the best opioids in the industry without the damning list of side-effects. I could lift the weight of fifty men, heal alarming wounds in mere moments. I had been in a fencing class down at the university for three years, going to several different teachers, going through several different forms of cutlery. The lightning would enhance whichever weapon I had on me at the time of transformation, allowing them to do incredible feats such as tale down a grove of trees in one horizontal swipe.

As I swam deeper and deeper into the darkness, light voices began to fill the ever-twisting cave system. I came to a bypass, the tunnel split into eight or nine different directions, all pitch black and empty. No sea life or plant life, just dark water. The voice called from a specific tunnel. The light singing and whispered called me like a symphony of sirens, but, when I faced the tunnel, a slightly larger opening than the other, I began to fall under a heavy spell of nauseous and vertigo. I could feel the energy pour out of me as I started to loss consciousness.

As my eyes closed, lungs filling with water, I began to think I'd be lost forever. The island would be lost to the ravenous imperialist invaders. While I hadn't seen much of my father lately, something told me he wouldn't be able to save the city in time. I couldn't disappoint Abi, Mal, father of all people. He once told me great men are either born great or either have greatness thrust upon them. I'm positive he plagiarized that from someone but either way I got the message.

I sank further, hitting the bottom of the chamber only to fall further into another opening, and despite being half unconscious I could feel the density in the water change. As I descend through the warm upper membranes of the strange yet familiar liquid, I realize where I am just as I loss complete consciousness, my mind drifts into the light.

....

I awaken at a wooden desk covered in otherworldly symbols, carved and scraped into the wood. Lifting up my head I'm startled by a classroom full of conversating students, sitting about on top of their desk and walking all completely unsupervised. No one turns to notice me in the back corner of the brightly lit room. I peek towards the front of the class and see that the chalkboard is also covered in unreadable script, complete with a very disturbing shade sketching of a solitary giant winged entity.

Sitting in a seat just in front of me to the left sits a familiar girl with her head in a book writing, undiscerned by the other students laughing and playing loudly around her. In the moment I spot her, the room falls silent, as my eyes take her in form head to toe. Her yellow rucksack hanging off her chair, the bag covered in graffiti all surrounded by her name in a fancy font. Delores.

"Delores." I whisper faintly as the room again becomes one overbearing yell. She doesn't hear me.

"Delores. "I reach for her again a little louder, she still writes unresponsive.

"I'm busy." She finally replies after a few moments of nothing. Her voice just as light as I remember. The room still engulfed in conversation and static around us.

Suddenly, feel something foreign inside my chest twist and snaps and I feel my stomach turn almost causing me to vomit. A great spell of nauseous and fatigue hits me like spoiled milk, my throat closes and start the gasp for air. The rest of the room becomes a silent grey fog and all I can see is her. I reach intensely for her aid, but no matter the strain she proves to be just out of arm's length. My eyes begin to close again as my heads slumps onto the vandalized desk, just before they do, her familiar voice awakens me.

"Feel like reading something for me?" Delores stand over my desk with a hand bent resting on her hip cocked to one side, holding out the notebook from before towards me. The sickness disappeared, I no longer felt as if I was slipping off a cliff. The shadow disappeared from the rest of the rest as my eyes began to adjust on her and the book she held in front of me.

"What's happening?" I joke calmly as the noise of the room returns as well. The book was covered in different colors and drawing interlaced with one another. She laughs.

"Well I switched over to writing recently, people were calling my sketchings dark so... read this for me, perhaps write me a review at the end or even a continuation if you deem so necessary, just deliver it back to me alright?" She explains before sliding the notebook under my arm atop the desk before returning to her seat. In confusion, I stare idle, unable to respond or react other than a faint shy confirmation after she'd already sat down.

I examine the front cover of the ragged journal, scribbled about the front, back and spine was a singular abstract coloring. It looked like the finger painting of an adolescent, dozens of colors spread across the book in no order or fashion at all. Upon opening the book, on the first page I spot her writings. At the top of the page read an odd title. 'The Light Bringer'.

It shot straight into an oddly written fantasy about an angel made entirely of light. This creature traveled infinitely through the cosmos, reigniting dead stars, washing planets of raging storms and bringing hope to desolate worlds everywhere in one form or another. Wherever it landed, life sprouted almost immediately beneath its feet, no matter how decayed and poisoned sat the ground. He was a cleanser of darkness, a bringer of life in places where life was previously impossible.

The story goes on the describe a gargantuan monstrosity that entered our universe through an accidently door being opened on the other side of the cosmos. The beast was so massive, it could not call any planet home in its birth system. Doomed to float space entirely, it fed on any planets and stars so unlucky to cross its aimless path. The being of light soon stumbles across a trail of worlds decimated by the beast and begins a steady chase.

Her writings begin to scramble into an unreadable mess, I'm lost. I can't put it on whether it's her handwriting, the thick ink, the paper, my eyes or my brain losing attention. I start to feel woozy, but I try to continue reading. Through the fog I start to notice descriptions to a galaxy that matches our own, nine base planets orbiting a young yellow sun, the third planet being the only habitable.

"What happened to him?" The pages are blank as I flip through looking for the conclusion.

"Are you familiar with Nirvana? It was the book that led your father to us. A great lightning bolt fell from the outer heavens, decimating the dinosaurs, kickstarting the ice age." Delores circles me oddly, her voice now low and very unfamiliar, it was no longer her but something else using her image. The room is empty, somehow, I hadn't noticed it'd been emptied.

"This too, be another tale of truth and power my Harry." Her voice has changed again, no longer do I hear her warming alto chords, replaced now by thousands of overlapping strange and unfamiliar voices.

The room dissipates like paper being burnt in high speed and I find myself floating weightlessly in an all-white limbo. I feel no clothes on my body, no temperature difference between the air and my skin. Floating, unattached completely. My eyes finally adjusted to the brightness of the purgatory. Silence echoes through the empty white hellscape. Below me I could see a spec of darkness, as I glared into its abyss it grew larger and it became known that I was staring out a window into star-littered swirling galaxy system. It began to zoom in greatly, zipping past thousands of planers, moons, suns and giant gas systems alike. Soon we came upon a familiar blue and green marble circling a bright yellow sun.

As I crept past Mars, I make out the mythic beast hovering just behind the sun. Its many tentacles and limbs caressing the star created a slim crescent of writhing shadow slowing enveloping the sun whole. Despite the blessed view id been given riding godly through the vacuum of space, I find myself cold as dread builds in my stomach and fear in my chest. A billion miles away and it trembles my core, hairs stand up on my neck as I find myself lost staring at the gigantic monster.

From the other side of the galaxy, a bright spec of blue and white zips t incredible speeds, zig zagging towards the monster like a bear on the hunt. Just as they make contact I am forced out of my trance as the moon obstructs my view, I realize I am still drifting towards Earth. Disappointed, I find solace in the silence and the dazzling lights bursting over the edge of the horizon like a water foundation sprinkled with dye.

Slowly I float down through the upper atmosphere, rolling fields of green dotted with shimmering lakes greeted me beautifully as the ground came closer. I come to an endless mixed grove of clementine trees and lemon trees. Mint lightly dotting the lush blanket of grass, embracing me as I float carelessly to the ground, the aisles of trees running forever in every direction, I find myself alone.

"We are beyond anything your civilization can describe, anything they can comprehend." Delores' distorted voice again speaks but she is nowhere to be found.

"What happened up there? Are you trying to tell me that story I just read was real?" I scream at only the rustling orange bushes lining each clementine tree.

"We sacrificed ourselves to defeat the evil that threatened this galaxy eons ago. The battle was unlike anything we'd ever faced, draining us completely. As the creature's corpse lie in front of us in a trillion pieces, we feel tired." I wander around the endless orange garden until I stumble across a pile of clementine's neatly stacked in the center of a circle of trees.

"Never had so such concentrated energy been exhausted in all the cosmos. The plummet was long and far, eventually falling into the blessed bosom of Gaia. The impact disintegrated the base consciousness we once were, bringing us to the brink of darkness. Our physical form seeped into the dirt, your island, was once and is a shining capital thanks to our blood running being sucked into its roots. Yet now, that capital sits in grave danger as does the rest of the universe." The pile of fruit catches fire in a puff a thick dark red and blue flames as I bend to grab one, knocking me on my rear and I catch a glimpse of New Shang set ablaze. The thick smoke plumes spiraled in different colors darkened by the ash as explosions continue to rock the already ruined cityscape.

"The capitals in trouble now, I need your help." I get up screaming again.

"While your city means nothing in the grand scheme, we grant you access to our infinite. For t was only mean we meet death that everything became clear, you are needed, grand monstrosities like the one in the story sit waiting just beyond the door or reality. This evil multiplied by infinity, idle at every closed window and opening, waiting for the chance to decimate all the lives in your realm. Save your people, then we will talk more." The voices stop as dark clouds roll quickly overheard and a storm forms. Lightning bolts begin to crack as rains pours heavily throughout the grove. Expecting a bolt of lightning to hit me, instead I get a slight tap on my right heel. One of the scorched clementines, blown loose by the wind. As I pick it up and dust it off, I realize its ice cold despite its burnt exterior. Still, I begin the peeling it as normal. Nothing seemed wrong with it at first, I had no doubts until a praying mantis appears from behind one of the wedges and jumps onto my shoulder.

I shudder for a moment, slowly and carefully trying to rid myself of the bug before I give up and begin hastily brushing my shoulders and torso, throwing the fruit down a few aisles in the process. Just then, I get hit in the back of the head with a piece of fruit, turning around expecting company I was met with again no one. I look to the ground the discarded fruit, the fruit I had half peeled and tossed away. How? It shocks me as I pick it up from the ground like the static shock of a balloon.

Unconvinced I was destined to bite into this strange fruit, I went ahead with it very nonchalantly, clearing the dust off a wedge and biting down hard. A surge of electricity shoots down into my core, bursting outward into every part of me as it reached my center. Cringing I shut my eyes in pain, upon opening them I find darkness rapidly enveloping the once beautiful grove. It devours me before I could react, I wake up and again find myself transported in the blink of my eye, this time back to drowning in the tunnel, back to reality, and back to the war.

“Death here is not an option Harold. Move. Your people await.” The voices speak one last time before I realize what’s happening.

I shoot out of the tunnels as fast as I could, and soon find myself headed towards an enemy firing across the southern border of the Nisha reef. Over forty battleships, cruisers and aircraft carriers, firing everything from heavy artillery to small side arms directly at me as if I had a big bright target painted on my back and front. For a few moments I hover menacingly, unsure of what to do or how to do it when I hear the dozens of voices scrambled into one from earlier.

“If you expect to defend your family, reach towards your enemies. Let them feel the everlasting warmth of your touch.” The voices laugh hardily before dissipating beneath the noise of the unwavering weaponry. I reach down towards the ships and a giant heavy stream of blue trimmed white light reaches down scorching the decks of the many ships. This goes on for a while, needlessly destroying every vessel that appeared in my eyeline.

"Don't forget your father." The voices return jokingly as if they weren't on my side. Still, I look towards the island, over the tree line far on the outskirts of New Shang. Through the unfamiliar dazzling glaze over my entire field of vision, I spot Edwin in the middle of a vineyards grape field. The swarm of bombers passing just overhead about to begin their bombing run. He raises his hand towards the still failing bombs, a spark of blue ignites at his fingertips as he aims high closing one eye to aim down his arm.

The spark explodes a dark red, encowling my father in the red blast and before I can even comprehend what has happened I break from the half-sinking fleet and whoosh across the island towards at the highest speed possible. Despite all of this, I see the warped crimson explosion burst again, and again, and again. Growing as it eats the vineyard and the front three row of bombers as they blindingly flew directly into the expanding mess.

Through the membrane of the fiery bubble I pierce like a swift dagger, the wonderous feeling of godhood erased immediately by the skin trembling sensation of oncoming death. I'd just been whipped across the galaxy yet those few miniscule moments of being completely consumed by fire really shook me, despite the barrier that protected me, the hairs on the back of my neck stood up.

Without blinking or stopping for even a moment I burst through the dark red and black flames and smoke, time slows, and Edwin comes into view again. Down on his knees, his arms hanging limb to his sides, his head cocked back with his mouth open and his eyes rolled back. I can only grab him fully, with both arms like a child I swoop him up from the ground and rush him out of the explosion beelining straight to Solitude and I hear the voices again.

"Close our eyes Harold, embrace us for a moment, embrace yourself." Time slows again, this time coming to a visually gorgeous halt. I float just over near the explosions most outer membrane, examining the colorful frozen fire hovering just over my shoulders.

"If you could stop time why didn't you tell me everything there was to tell me at once back in the caverns. Did you see what just happened to him?!" I look down at him before screaming out to space.

"Look at him, so weak and aging, his time clearly behind him. The better part of his life was spent on just finding this sacred island. It's time for him to face his nirvana."

"What are you going on about? The book, I'll read it I swear, now let me get him to his home so he can be healed. I'll read it to him as he recovers I promise, please you have to unfreeze time, tell me how to stop this, now!

Please, please you have to just let me take him home. I can heal him, right?" Again, I look down at him, the protective plasma around me has enveloped him as well. Loose strands of fire trailing off his face back into the still painting that was the frozen wall of fire.

"You are willing to let his failure destroy a better part of your homeland? Sure, the landscape will regrow overnight, but the lives lost are lost Harold. Taking him home ensures nothing but more destruction as the remaining navy boards the island and begins massacring your people. You are willing to ignore the remaining bombers when you know Ali cannot finish them alone. These other humans aim to wipe your people from this island and claim us for their own wicked agendas. We will not allow evil to possess our power, our anciency must be protected Harold. Your father knew this, his blinding dedication brought him to this point. This is the toll of obsession and power. The loyalty he installed must not die with him Harold."

"Stop saying it's the end we can heal him, right? Why do you keep ignoring that?'

"The waters will heal any physical wounds, but humans are so complex. Once the brain is damaged, memory is lost. Many basic functions aren't revived when the brain is put back together. He can recover but he will cease to be the father you once knew. He would be a vegetable doomed to..."

"And what do you suggest." I interject sneering my teeth as tears began building in my eyes. "Let his family at least bury him."

"Take his physical form and do with as you please, but save your people first, correct your fathers last mistake. Once that is done, his fate will be realized." A moment passes as we loom over Edwin.

"Alright." I wipe my face before looking around at the scene still frozen, bombers stuck hanging as bombs sit quietly unexploded stuck in space. The vineyard mostly encompassed by the explosion, the surrounding farms and houses just catching fire from the intense heat.

"How do we do this." I ask myself, thinking the voices had gone away. I look again at an unconscious Edwin, his veins glowing a bright blue.

"Let us take over." The voices quickly silence me before time unfreezes slowly. The forces take over as rapidly I begin circling the circumference of the sphere, the trailing lightning behind me tightening and constricting around the bubble as if to gain sentience. Edwin still in my arms as I head for the top of the now purple sphere of lightning and fire I circled, dragging behind all the essence of the gas and fire as the explosions immediately evaporated into the dozens of simmering lightning ropes. Smoke plums from the collapsing wraps as the bands shrank into a tiny trail behind me as again I headed towards the remain bombers and again I feel in control. I zig zag through each airplane, ripping through the wings and engines as if they were clouds, and with a smoking string a falling craft behind me I continue South, repeating the same headfirst maneuvers with remaining navy ships.

Once I finish the ships, I turn towards the island when I look down at Edwin, laying still yet now illuminating even brighter. Again, the voices intervene as the chaos dies below us floating about two hundred meters off the ground.

"Release him from your world Harold. End his human suffering and in the process become stronger yourself."

"I... can't. I'm not ready to do this."

"You risk dragging out his decay, his torture, your families torture. He already stands with one foot in the grave as your people would say. One touch to his temple will release his consciousness into the great void. Bury him in a grand tomb befitting to his honor. He discovered fire, not Prometheus. The flame he has lit must be preserved, his torch is passed to you on this day and on this day alone Harold. Fate knocks."

I examine my trembling hand glowing with power, the index finger pointed out like a gun right next to Edwin's forehead, his right temple, the effects of the power coursing so wildly through my veins I hadn't even noticed. I contemplate ending Edwin now, ending my mother's worrying about his health, as with Ali. All my loved ones, stressed constantly on his state of mind, his wellbeing, the people around him. Everyone safety was in jeopardy if he roamed free, and as I pondered the voices continued, listing reason after reason how this would build my character, how they could easily do this for me, but it must be a choice of free will. Horse shit, all of it. I could tell there was some vita piece of information they were conveniently leaving out, what do you want with me.

As I continue to wonder, I realize the voices hear me dwelling in doubt and paranoia.

"Your father will die in the public eye a hero, who went out protecting his homeland. You will not only succeed him, but you are the one who is destined to guide us across the universe once again. He was but the messenger, you are the god. His mission complete, deliver him to his nirvana."

Tears building heavily in my eyes as I move my index finger pointed towards his skull even closer. Smoke still billowing around us in the distant as thunder rumbles behind the darkened clouds. Yelling loudly skyward, I prepare myself to pull the metaphysical trigger, when I feel a tug at my waist.

I look down in surprise, Edwin, with an ounce of life one eye opens slightly and he whispers forcing me to lean in. In leaning in I brush his head with my finger and a shot of lightning blasts through his skull like a bullet, I catch only two words before the accidental shot cuts him short. I weep in agony, we fall out of the sky and land in a field of burning aircraft wreckage when rain starts to pour heavily despite never having rained since my time here. Thunder again cracks as I ponder his final words to me. “Fate lies.”

Sunlaverian Public News Access Tape 334-P

Reporter on Scene: Adam Walton

Camera: Jacob Kingston

A reporter in a grey suit stands in front of a large hall structed in Greek columns and bordering. He looks off screen to the cameraman waiting for the signal to go behind him a sea of other reporters and spectators. After a few awkward moments of dead-air he speaks in a loud clean English accent.

"Adam Walton here, outside the main entrance of the Vizanti hall. Chancellor Hebrank has just stepped out of an hours long press conference with the council as wells as the various heads of state and media." He pauses to look over the exciting crowd, cheering as a hooded female being escorted by dark shaded suits out of the hall.

"Hundreds are out today as well to see the first public appearance of Ali in over two years ago. Sources on Solitude Island tell us she's been hidden away in the Southern Forest since the death of our beloved, rumored to be doing anything from training, painting, gardening or hunting, who knows. For the viewers that can't recall the incident that occurred in what is now Helios Park in the Southern outskirts of New Shang. The discoverer and founding father of Sunlatveria was gravely injured in a botched defensive attack against invading Japanese forces."

For a moment the camera man pans to the left of Walton on the roaring crowds, waving various signs in both agreement and protest, all chanting an inaudible thunderous rabble. Anti-Japanese signs as well 'go away foreigners' signs. There were more posters of admiration for the Hebrank family than anything else. Walton continues as the camera again focuses.

"Despite the horrific tragedy that occurred on the ground, it was a different story in the sky. Native Islander, Ali, single-handily downed over two dozen enemy planes before they could even cross the Corinthian River. I know we all remember that day as a dreary day in Sunlatverian history but we as a people have rebuilt and continued forward. The passing of our nations founder will forever we etched into our memories. Moving forward, a few months ago Harold brought forth the first draft of his new constitution, the final draft is set to go into effect today."

The crowd roars a mix of love and hate, the camera moves to the entrance to see Louise fitted with two black suited bodyguards and ten public guards pushing back the mob of journalists, adoring fans and activist.

"First Daughter Louise steps out, beautiful as ever. Louise was groomed to one day take the dying despots thrown, but due to Harold's arrival to the island only a few years ago, she was cast aside by our father. Harold took notice and has said to appoint her as First Advisor. Advising and guiding Harold as he steps to the thrown as well as being appointed Ethics General, overseeing all moves and decisions of the new Vizanti senate as well as its new inner cabinet." The camera follows Louise as she is escorted into the center car of a five-car motorcade.

"Louise will also be heading the new Judiciary committee established within the new Vizanti senate. A true believer in her father and his legacy, Louise has always been the voice of the Sunlatverian people one hundred percent." The camera focuses again on our familiar well-dressed reporter.

"Another big-ticket item on this new constitution is the establishing of a national military, one focused solely on homeland defense. This new army will cover mainly all three aspects of defense. Land, sea, air. As well as a national draft based on a specific set of baselines yet revealed to the public." He again turns to the crowd as another figure exits the hall, this one void of an entourage. The crowd cheers harder, louder than before.

"And Chancellor Hebrank steps out, also declaring today that he is taking the Solidius title from today forward in honor of our former leader. More importantly, the chancellor has disbanded the International Vizanti council. For those at home that don't know, Sunlaveria has always been run by a coalition of International diplomats due to a treaty signed in the republic's first years. He will be replacing the council with a one house senate derived from publicly elected officials from various districts, headed by him and a cabinet of senate appointed specialties. This news is cause for celebration for most across Sunlatveria tonight, but many claim exclusion from this new constitution." The crowd fades as a streak of light flashes out the camera for a second followed by a loud crack of thunder.

"And there he goes people, your new Supreme Chancellor. Dangerously zipping of into the distance to somewhere, we don't know. More on this story and how it develops tonight. Back to you Brendan."

The camera fades off as the noise of the roaring crowd dies in black and white. "Seems unnecessary if you ask me." Walton says before if finally clicks out.

Chapter 4

The Third Sun

196X

New York City. Somewhere in the lower section of the Bronx borough underneath a rumbling trainline. The time is late, the night sky starless as a light mist fogs the area cutting visibility down drastically. A hooded caricature about five feet five inches, leans against a support column taking a long drag from a shoddily rolled cigarette. His focus across the grimy street to a pawn shop sporting a huge wooden sign that read ‘BEST PAWN’ in bright pink letters bordered in gold. A black female sporting purple lip liner and jet-black hair employee inside closing the place as other employees take off through the main entrance.

She locks the glass doors behind her coworkers as they take off.

The hooded individual flicks his cigarette as the last witnesses on the street disappear. Lazily he drags himself across the street with ill-intent in his eye as a heavy downpour of rain begin out of nowhere. He pounds on the glass with one hand while the other hides in his pocket, pleading for the woman to let him in before he gets soaked. She looks up from counting a pile of bills to see the malnourished bum trying to get her attention. The name tag pinned to her pink and gold stripped shirt read 'Airica'. She tries to wave him away, mouthing was closed but he persists, beating harder on the glass as the rain fell heavier as he ignores her suggestion.

Afraid he'd bring down the door, she scurries to stuff all the bills into the drawer, making sure to lock it before she made her next move. Slowly she approaches the door, stealthily grabbing a pair of scissors from behind the counter as she came around the corner, motioning for him to step back as she approached. Ignoring her instruction, he continues beating the glass with one hand and it starts to crack and she begins to scream at him to take a step back.

The maniac brandishes a snub nose pistol from his pocket and begins slamming the barrel repeatedly into the crack he'd created trying to expand it. She presents the scissors as a defense strategy, threatening him as he continued, tears beginning to build in her eyes from a mix of sheer terror, confusion, shock.

Thunder rumbles in the skies above as the storm crashes harder and harder into the city. Lightning flashes behind the thick clouds, illuminating the crazed man from behind terrifying the girl to the point where she runs back to the counter and grabs the phone. Frazzled, shaking, unable to calm herself she tries to dial for the police when she notices something outside the shop behind the lunatic attempting to break in. A tall caped with broad shoulders individual appears in the flash of a lightning bolt standing across the street facing the degenerates back. Another flash of lightning burst through the sky above, the thunder shaking the building. The man seemingly teleports from across the street to directly behind the assailant still trying to bash his way into the shop.

The woman slowly puts down the phone as the dial tone dies out, caught in the horrific scene unfolding before her as again the lightning strikes and the second man disappears. The fanatic stops his assault as if he'd sensed the man's presence behind him. Turning to find no one, he continues terrorizing the girl inside the shop. Again, the thunder booms, lightning flashes and a bolt as thick as a light pole crashes atop the man, bursting through his head and down the center of his torso. Another flash cracks in the sky and the second man appears again standing where he stood before, just behind the bum as his smoking now hollowed corpse falls to the wet ground headless.

A horrified smile lurches across her face as she rushes to open to door excitedly.

"Harold!" She screams as she wraps her arms around his waist.

"Hey Peg. How ya been sweet cheeks?" He replies wrapping his arms around her head and shoulders, kissing the top of her head.

"You didn't have to kill the crazy bastard." She says softly looking down at the scorched corpse.

"Don't tell me you had it under control, with those dull things." He jokes motioning down to the scissors in her hand, her grip loosens, dropping the scissors to the ground.

"I did as a matter of fact. What are you doing here anyway Harold, and what were you thinking making an entrance like that. I appreciate the help but that was overkill sweetie." She pulls away, her smile fades quickly as she rushes back into the store to escape the downpour. "I mean what am I supposed to do about this mess anyway, between him and the door ready to fall off, not only will I get fired I'll be in prison for the rest of my natural life. I have a son to think about for fucks sake."

"Relax babe." He follows her through the door, wiping the rain from his face. "I'll handle the big pieces. The rain will wash away the rest. I saw trying to get in with a gun, protecting you was the first thing that came to mind." She goes back to closing the shop, hurriedly locking the drawers before she begins to scribble on a piece of paper. “Now speaking our son, he’s the reason I’m here. How’s he doing.”

“He’s doing as you expected, great in school, its after school I have the problem with. These streets aren’t safe Harold, I dream of the day we can move to New Shang with you.”

She hurries through her closing duties before grabbing her brown leather purse and a matching brown overcoat off a rack in the far corner of the store.

“Outside, come on.” She pushed Harold into the rain before putting on her coat and doing her best the lock the front door to its now wobbly frame. “Clean up your mess now, and can you try to not leave a trail of bodies leading right to my doorstep?”” She motions to the hollowed husk laying in front of the windows. He turns his head over towards the carcass before reaching out his left arm, a spark of electricity ignites in his extended hand and focuses into a stream of energy towards the large pieces of the mutilated man. One by one he blasted the pieces into smaller bits, the rain flooding it all into a nearby sewer opening.

“I’ll try.” He finally responds as he finishes cleaning up the mess. He turns back to the woman who is already half way down the block, strutting quickly around a corner. Harold rushes up to her in a blink, flapping his cape to free it of all retained water before attempting to use it as an umbrella over her head. He examines her uniform, spotting the nametag.

"Airica? Only name tag they had left?" He asks as they briskly race towards a train station halfway down the empty block. The volley of rain still battering the street, the sound of all the car roofs being beat upon by the downpour was heavy.

"Yeah, she didn't need it anymore." They duck into the subway, the attendant on duty staring up from his magazine in disbelief at the man in a full suit of black armor.

"So why are you Harold? Its been what, four-five years since you last checked in? Not so much as a letter, a phone call. For fucks sake I see shit about Sunlatveria every once and again on the news but come on." She sighs heavily stepping away from him, her eyes frozen locked on one green tile amongst a sea of tan on the floor. Grabbing some tokens from her bags, she plucks the nametag off, dumps it in the trash and continues through the turnstiles.

"Peggy wait!" Harold rushes behind her, for split second his physical form shifts into a cloud of smoke and blue and white lightning resembling a pair of floating snakes or dragons. Phasing through the turnstile machine, in a blink he his beside her in complete physical form. The attendants mouth drops as does his reading material as he gets up and rushes out of the station as fast as possible.

"Yeah I've come to take him alright. But I need you to listen to me." She sits down under a big anti-Sunlatveria propaganda poster. It was all red with a dark painted man attacking a cowering family with a bolt of lightning. He takes the seat besides her under the misinformation as she fiddles her finger waiting on the train. The subway platform nearly empty except a homeless man on one of the opposite platforms and a young couple sitting closing to the entrance, too busy giggling into each other's necks to notice their surroundings.

"What happened to Alice? Is everything alright at home?" She asks looking up at him worriedly.

"Everybody is fine. Well not everybody, Ellis is sick. And Louise is refusing the lake on his behalf, as she always has. It used to be admirable, but now, I just see it as stubborn stupidity." He replies staring off over the tracks, his hands fall in between his legs clasped as he slumps against the bench. "I just want her to realize what she's doing to him, what I could do for him."

"You feel for her husband. But in what way Harold? He held no political seats in the Vizanti am I right? He was a philanthropist business man yes but what was he in the bigger picture? As someone who as seen the edge of the universe, I'd think you'd have a better sense of scale when it came to love."

He sighs before rubbing the back of his head, bringing it over and down his face in one motion.

"Does Ali know?" She asks before turning her head towards the train tunnel.

"Of course, I mean she does her own things and I mean we do a lot together. I mean you remember whenever you'd come down." He smiles before nugging her elbow. "I mean do you remember the shit we'd get into, geez." They both laugh for a moment before silence again takes the stage.

"An-anyway, the Vizanti council is the reason I'm here. Someone leaked to the Sunlatverian press that I'm harboring a child in the States. It looks bad on me and our countries current stance on the US. They're blockading all western trade to us right now, did you know that? Anyway, its times he met his real family, he has a birthright ready to be claimed."

"Don't disrespect me as if I'm not his real family, or that the people here don't mean anything. He's old enough to know when he's being played Harold, and I'm am not the same young woman who you used to hypnotize with your fancy magic. I don't give a shit about politics or trade blockades, you're not taking him!" She gets up and moves down the platform as the sound of the approaching train picks up.

Behind him as he stands up, a small squad of policeman enter the turn-stiles to investigate a mysterious and panicked call about a possible Sunlatverian.

"FREEZE!" Someone screams as they spot the rouge despots flailing cape. Calmly he turns toward them, the train gaining on the station.

"What crime did I commit officers?" He asks softly but loud enough for them to hear as he slowly begins raising his arms.

"Put your hands on your head and get on your knees, now!" One of the officers' yell, his voice shaking, nearly cracking at one point. The gaggle of Caucasian officers all stood in various positions of ready with their guns drawn and aimed on Harold.

"I am a foreign dignitary from the state of Sunlatveria. I must be granted some sort of diplomatic immunity for just existing."

"Aint no goddamn diplomatic immunity. Were taking you in, dead or alive Solidius." Another officer says, this one sterner and deeper. "We hit the jackpot tonight boys."

"Like finding Castro in your kitchen."

"Hell yeah. They are gonna promote every one of us, give us all medals. I can finally retire early like I've always dreamed."

"Mchale, radio to Jacobs, tell him to get all of his guys together and get here now."

"On it." The younger officer activates his radio, informing them of who'd they found, where and what train he was waiting for.

The leading officer steps forward smoking a cigarette.

"Ever since it hit the fan that your kid was somewhere in the city, every cop from here to Hoboken has been looking for 'em. Top to bottom. Figured whoever we were looking for was dead by now, or maybe you'd already come and whisked him off in the rain. But look at you, still searching… and of all places, you're here, in my jurisdiction." The office gets closer and closer and Harold lowers to his knees.

"Where anything can happen." Another officer follows up from behind snickering softly.

The train passes as he puts his hands fully in the air and something about the train coinciding with his movement spooks one of the older policeman and he lets off a shot.

The leading officer drops to the ground slowly, bloods building up across his shirt front and spewing slowing from his mouth.

"Mackey you idiot!"

"Dammit I didn't mean to fuck!"

"Shit man you really screwed the fucking pooch on that one, wait 'til we tell the captain you shot the Sarge in his back."

"It was an accident man really, look, let's just blame it on captain plasmo over there."

"That's all fine and dandy, except them Sunlatverians don't use bullets."

"Yeah it's all blades or some lightning energy bullshit." Using the distraction, Harold phases into the cloud of dueling energy serpents and in a micro second, he shoots behind the officers, forming back into his physical self except both hands were small curved sickles of dazzling light, already jabbed deep within the spines of the two closest men.

"Sometimes it's a funny mix of both." He smiles and cackles as he rips the blades out with a spin of blood of sparkling electricity. The two men flip and fall to the ground as the remaining open fire in terrified awe and horror.

"Don't worry, youll love." Harold says looking down at the two men bleeding from their sides.

Again, he phases into energy, the bullets pass through the cloud, ricocheting off the tiled wall behind him, one of the bullets nicks one of the officers in the neck and he drops like a bag of potatoes, blood spouting widely. Harold materializes again, this time directly in front of the remaining four officers, his left-hand forms into the head of a sledge hammer and he knocks the man across the tracks to another platform, smacking him up against a center column.

"You Americans..." He knocks another of the men with his hammer, sending the man flying into another officer running up, both fall into the tracks in their confusion.

"I was once one of you!" The hammer phases out and his fist begins to glow as he throws a few quick jabs at another officer, the lightning twisted around his fingers scorching the officers clothing and skin with each punch. "This was my home!" He continues as his rages begins to boil.

"I am not the enemy!" He comes up on an officer already on his knees begging for forgiveness. With a swift roundhouse kick, Harold boots the man into the train tracks but not without first smashing against the tunnel wall and an advertisement for cheese.

"YOU ARE!!!" He yells before smashing the last mans head in with the hammer, his right hands forms into a second blunt object as he pounds the mans brains into the cracking platform. The train finally stopped, and the doors open, he looks up from the mess, the young couple already gone, scared by the initial arrival of the cops. The bum on the opposite platform hiding under his newspaper. Peggy on the brightly lit train, clasped against one of the poles staring at Harold.

"You coming? My stops about an hour and a half away." She yells, snapping him from his violent trance.

"I-I could fly us there faster." He says catching his breath as he enters the empty train car and takes a seat in front of her.

"It's raining. Plus, now they know you're in town. I don't really want to broadcast where I live to the whole city."

"If you heard what he said. Then you heard the part about them looking for Rex, it's time for me to take him." She looks away down the train sighing.

"You knew, didn't you? You knew that information had leaked." He stands and approaches her in confusion. She turns from him again. "You leaked it! Didn't you!"

"Yeah it was me, so what?!" She turns back to him angry, face red. "You abandoned us Harold, here, in this shit city. While you and your other family live in a fucking castle on your own island?! I was there for you in the beginning, before you had all of that and all of this." She motions at his suit. "You were a normal guy who cared about me, school, his sister, his mom. You were a better man when you were simple, when you were mine and mine alone." She turns again, crossing her arms.

"Peg." He turns her around by the shoulders. "I love you, I always have. But you risked the safety of our child when you leaked that information."

"Don't give me that shit Harold, you risked the safety of our child when you left him and his mother in one of the most crime ridden cities in the world."

"This was my city to at one point. I believed it would make him stringer I thought it'd be better if he grew up outside of my families influence."

"What the fuck ever Harold, take your fucking son. Leave me here like you always do and just take your fucking kid. Just get me home in one piece and never show up in my life again you hear me?!" They both sigh and their eyes never connect again, both staring aimlessly down opposite ends of the train.

An hour passes of stop after stop of mostly deserted platforms, the few lonely riders who do hop aboard are greeted by a silver-streaked man comfortably unwinding open legged across two seats. The knight in black fitted armor isn't enough to send them running, they board and get off at their usual stops without delay or fuss. Soon the train slows as another station comes into view, revealing multiple platforms lined with dozens upon dozens of waiting cops.

"How many more stops?" He whispers, the engineer speaker blares something inaudible, alerting everyone in the underground station of their arrival.

"This is the last one on the train, we have to hop on that one on the far platform." She points across four tracks, each lined with gawking officers readying their pistols and shotguns towards the pair.

"Once those doors open, take cover in the operators' booth. When you see an opening, get to that platform as fast as you can."

"I'm usually stuck waiting on that train for hours, what are we going to do Harold. Im not as spry as I used to be."

"Don't worry." He starts caressing the top of the pole and the ceiling of the car with his hand as he moves towards the door. "It's coming, now get ready, and you still look damned good to me by the way." He kisses her quick on the forehead before turning back towards the door.

"You saw what he did to our boys over at Gunhill, take no chances, empty your clip the second the spot him."

The rickety doors slide open slowly and immediately one the cops notice him in his bulking suit of armor.

"Over here!" He yells before shots begin flying from every direction. He shifts into the cloud of smoke laced with dancing electric eels as his essence blasted through the closest man like a hand propelled rocket. The bullets passing through him like gel as his forms neither bled nor flinched.

Peg dives to the floor of the platform behind them, ducking behind a bench waiting for an opportunity to rush up the stairs and around to her waiting platform. A cloud of concrete dust picks up from the floor as the officers continue spraying wildly hoping to hit the mysterious assailant.

"Stop him!" A dozen officers of the hundred scream in unison.

They try. They empty clip after clip as Harold dancing between the streams of the bullets, shooting himself from one victim to the next. Going in and out of physical form in flashes blinding the surrounding platforms, attacking each cop individually with graceful accuracy beyond anything they'd ever seen. Snapping an arm, poof into a cloud of smoke of buzzing electricity and towards the next foe, poof, again stands the knighted man with a crouching jab straight into to another officers' stomach.

The officer bends over groaning as again the man transforms into dust in the blink of an eye. The officer starts shooting wildly hoping to land a shot in the fog, only hitting another officer down the track in the shoulder. Again, the man materializes, this time behind the officer turning in shock as his neck is quickly snapped. Another body hits the floor as Harold jumps off the platform, transforming midair into the sentient cloud and continuing his spree of provoked terror.

Back on the original platform, Peggy spots on an opportunity to get around to the next train. Cautious she moves from the bench, to a column, to a trash can and up the stairs, all crouching and as silently as she could. Cops still firing aimlessly across the terminal, she had to be careful.

"Southbound to Coney, Southbound to Coney, Arrival in three minutes." An automated voice blares over the stations loudspeaker.

Some curious officer spots the dark-skinned woman pussyfooting around the active warzone and move to apprehend her, catching Harold's eye as they corner her at the top of the stairs on the walkway. Abandoning mid-swing the decapitation of another officer already on his knees begging for mercy, Harold shifts into the cloud bursting forward again as the twin flying snakes of light blue and shimmering white.

The serpents shoot up the stairs about four feet off the ground in such a rush it scatters the debris littered across the poorly swept floors of the station. As three police man surround the woman, one grabs her arms twisting it, forcing her lower to the ground. One of the men spots the rapidly approaching pair of beings of begins firing down the staircase, the bullets passing in between the mystic reptiles surrounding in an aura of rippling static. Harold forms again at the top of the stairs, bullets ricochet off his chest plate as he immediately out of the cloud he impales the closest officer in the eye with a long-jagged blade made of solidified electricity.

The others jump back, Harold extracts the blade and swipes horizontally and in one motion slits the throats the men before they can fall back further. Blood splatters across the floor, staining Peggy's egg white heels as she comes to her feet with his assistance. She peers down the stairs, listening as through the chatter and agony of the surviving officers still across the subway, she hears the approaching train.

"That's our train right, and were home safe?" Harold asks looking down the way anxiously as the surviving cops begin gathering their resources and radioing in for reinforcements.

"We aren't safe until we see the water." She adds turning back to him smiling as she plants a kiss of his chin. Nervously she scans the station as sirens can now be heard coming from street level. "The water is home."

The trains creeps up and screeches to a halt, our dynamic couple rush on board, Harold turns towards the inrushing cops blasting out quick bolts with his right hand, blocking bullets with the armor or his left hand. Peg ducks behind the seats as the train conductor bursts through his cabins and flees the station in a hurry.

"Shit wasn't the guy?" Harold ask still blocking shells as he looks over to Peg for a moment.

"I got it." Without thought, Peg rushed into the cabin and gets the doors closed and the train moving in no time and again they find themselves lurching through a dark tunnel.

"How far?" Harold says catching his breath as he leans against the threshold of the cabin.

"About thirty minutes, I'm not stopping til I see Coney so we should be good lest they block the tracks.

"They're not that smart." He sighs. "Peg, I want you to come to the island with us. Ill set you up in a nice spot on the outskirts of New Shang."

"Thanks, but no thanks Harold. Thank your son and go, don't throw your pity my way. Without him I guess I'll be free to get out of New York finally. Been here my whole life, I'm ready to see something else. Not Sunlatveria either." She says her eyes focused on the track.

"Why not? There is no pity, I love you." Harold's exclaims taking the free seat behind her.

"I'm not uprooting my life, so I can be your mistress Harold. Fuck that and fuck you. I know you're in love with Ali, I don't know how she was married to your father for like three decades but okay, sure, whatever Harold. Anyway, I don't need or your royalty."

He sighs. "Abi's dead. And Mal is sick. Refusing any lake treatments. Right now, it's just me and Louise running things. I need him alright; his sister needs him.

She turns to him, placing a hand on his knee. “That’s horrifying. I didn’t know. I’m so sorry Harold. What happened?”

“Terror attack a few years ago in the capital.”

“And your mother?”

“Cancer.”

“Jeez, I’m so sorry Harry. I loved them both so much.” She slowly turns back forward to the tracks. “And Ali?”

“Raising Alice in the mountain West of Solitude. Keeping her out of the spotlight until she’s a bit older.”

“I miss them all so much, I’ve yet to meet Alice, she must be a beautiful little girl.”

“She is Peg. And yeah, Abi loved you.” He pauses to sigh for a moment catching a tear preemptively. “Look the offer stands as long as the island does. You’re always welcome alright?”

“Thanks Harold, but before I left the States, I’d like to...”

“You’d like to what?” Harold waits for her to finish her sentence but looks up and out of the window and sees what has her stumped. They break from the tunnel as they begin over a bridge, a squad of six military helicopters moving over the water towards the train. The rain was gone, a thick fog replaced it, blanketing the city and the water around them.

"Shit, they're going to blow the bridge to get rid of you." The helicopters slow as the reach the bridge just ahead, all lining up in a row.

"I don't think they're aiming for the bridge Peg." In each chopper sits a gunner on a big machine gun, the guns begin to whirl, and bullets begin the shred the top of train.

"Keep the train moving forward!" Harold screams before bursting upward through the ceiling of the metal train car, landing atop the roof of the front car.

"Leave us alone!" He screams as he begins to slowly wade his arms around his as if he was swimming or doing karate moves at half speed. Around him sparks begin to ignite midair, wave of electricity begins pouring into from everywhere around him including the train itself. Up above dark clouds begin to swirl and as extends his arms to the sky, six gigantic bolts of lightning fly down, destroying the helicopters in single strikes each. The train swiftly passes underneath as the flaming wreckages fall into the river below all in unison.

"Harold get down here!" Peg screams for the car below, Harold looks down to see a policeman, holding her hostage, dragging her towards the back of the train, car by car.

He leaps into the hole he'd created just as the train finishes the bridge and goes into another tunnel. He begins marching towards the scared officer who must've hidden aboard the train at the last stop, the cop fires wildly at Harold through at least two empty train cars hitting nothing but metal and glass.

Finally, Harold corners him in the caboose as the train screeches and rumbles, the officer reloads his clip still aiming at Harold but hesitates, hiding behind Peggy.

"Coney is the end of the line, once we get there, there's nowhere for this train to go. This train is going full speed, you'll die, she'll die. I won't. Let her go, maybe we stop this train, maybe you go home tonight."

"Unlike the dozens of officers, you slaughtered tonight!" The officer yells, face full of red, before again firing wildly, emptying his clip.

Harold materializes a shield, blocking the bullets without effort. Shells ricochet throughout the train, shattering more glass as Harold lifts his arm, pointing his finger like a gun and fires a quick stream, blasting right through the mans eye poking over Pegs shoulder. Peg and the twitching dead man fall to the grand in a thud, Harold rushes to catch Peg before she hits the ground.

"Peggy? What's wrong?" Her face is cold, her eyes listing. He looks down, his hands covered in blood, unsure of who's blood. He lifts up her shirt to see an entry wound of one of the strays, turning her, he finds no exit wound.

“Can you fix me?” She says barely conscience.

“Of course, lets…”

“Wait.” She interrupts. “Don’t. Its cold Harry, just hold me for a minute okay? No powers, no paradise. Just us for this last moment, please?” She smiles softly up and him who smiles backs, light tears breaking in both their eyes as they embrace as he stays silent.

“I love you.” She whispers.

The train lurches forward with a big crash as it hits the boundary of the final station. The front train explodes as the remaining cars plummet into the former, the impacting explosion flips train cars into every direction through the train station ripping it apart. Harold holds her as tight as he can as their car flips into the fiery mayhem.

After a few moments, their car, half demolished and scorched to hell comes to halt atop the bonfire of another car. Harold manages footing and stands with the burnt corpse of his former lover still clutched in his arms. Again, he weeps lightly surrounded by hell as her corpse crumbles into ashes and hunks.

Chapter 5

Operation Highjump

194X

Found Journal of Lieutenant Junior Grade Allen Woods

December 8th

Karalyn, I count the seconds until this war is finished and I can finally go home. After so much energy the world as put into extinguishing these Nazis, we all deserve a break from the fighting but not so. The last date entry is 1944, I haven't written in a while, I know, I'm sorry. We've been docked near Elephant Island since Summer, waiting for orders to come through about what to do next. They should be coming in any day now according to the captain. Rumors are floating around the ship on why we're all the way out here, the war ended last year, and we haven't been in a scuffle in months. They're saying there's some hidden Nazi research base inland Antarctica, others are saying its Soviet.

Captain insists it's some training exercises on the ice, his guess is we must be preparing for a Russian homeland invasion, but even he isn't confident in his answer. From the research I've done on the Russians I shudder at the idea. I just focus on getting home to the warm comfort of good old Illinois. Lots of guys here from all over, I think only two or three other Ensigns are from our neck of the woods.

There's this one engineer from some island called Sunlatveria, never even heard of it before but he says we're pretty close to it from where we're stationed at the moment. Says he travelled to the stated to enlist after it became public was they were doing in Germany, he was originally from Poland, but he moved to Sunlatveria back in the early thirties because as he claims he could see the monster rising in Europe.

Like I said before, I know I haven't written much. I promised I'd bring you back this journal full of stories for your studies and I haven't. I truly apologize, let's hope that before I come home, I can fill this thing with one more good tale for ya. Happy birthday by the way, I hope the kids are treating you well. Hey, listen to that, Admiral just blared over the loudspeaker, orders came through, everyone report to the main deck for briefing. Shit, its cold up there Karalyn. Colder than I ever felt before. Whole damn ship is like an icebox. I hope he makes it quick. At least they gave us some thick parkas, I'll talk to you later love.

December 27th

Hey babe, how're you doing today? How're the kids and the rest of the family? How was Christmas? Tell everyone I said Merry Christmas, daddy will be home soon. I'm ready to come home Karalyn, I'm beyond ready. Just before Christmas, orders stated we had to embark on a journey through the cold. Acting as Marines, they strapped us up best they could in the latest experimental thermal wear and sent seven squads from my ship as well as seven from the six surrounding ships on this little excursion through the snow.

I welcome and long for the hidden warmth of a Chicago winter compared to days trekking this frozen wasteland. I'm haunted by memories of us playing atop the ice as we did so many years ago. Tonight, we camp in a giant cavern of ice and frost, Captain and Central are tight lipped on why we're out here, why we've been out here for days. They made each individual squad bring along some standout research scientist and another intelligence lackey. They kept to themselves, took notes whenever we stopped, they carry their own weight so that's okay with me.

Rumors with the rest of the crew insist on were looking for a Nazi or a Soviet base, I guess we'll see. The techs said were less than a day's trek from the final rally point, we meet up with B company at rally point bravo and await further orders from Central. That's all I know but I can feel it in my gut, something big is about to go down. If not, well I'd be real disappointed, I mean making us walk days in ice cold temperatures for nothing would just grind my gears.

God my hands are freezing up, this cold is nothing like home. I'll talk to you later babe. The sky is so beautiful now, calm and clear.

January 4th

We're holed up atop a glacier a few clicks from the South Pole. Getting ready to head back to the ships. A lot of shit went down, stuff I'd never thought I'd see in a billion years Karalyn. I'm scared for you, for all of us. Rumors were right on the money. Nazi stronghold, a big castle made of stone and metal built atop an ice cavern, bigger than any fortress I'd ever seen. That wasn't the horror, it was at first but that was soon over shadowed.

Despite catching them surprise, they managed to Pin us down quick, way more firepower than there needed to be at a place so remote. Those walls were so damned thick, our demolition crews tried dozens of times we just couldn't get through. We only managed to get to this point safely because of he untimely arrivals of the Russians. I guess they got the same intel we did and headed down to see what the fuss is about.

About a hundred thousand Russians poured over the hill, tanks, bombers, fighters, the works. Biggest ground assault I'd seen throughout the entirety of the war. God knows how they got here so fast, but they saved us for e moment. Before they started fucking everything up. The bombers and fighters started making their runs, but the bombers were off by huge marks, missing on purpose it seemed, creating huge cracks in the ice around the entire area. The landscape began to shake and tremble greatly, so we began firing on the Russian bombers with small arms just to get them to stop. They took this the wrong way and the fighter began running through us for a while as their other assaults continued.

That's when the sky turned dark and the winds picked up. A huge blizzard moved in out of nowhere, in what seemed like the blink of an eye.

Through the snow I could see streak of lightning raining down across the Russians as cracks of thunder burst through the loud wind around us. Above the Nazi fortress I could make out a man in all black armor, followed by a long cape whipping in the winds. The man hovered as bullets from below bounce off him in every direction, unmoved by the attacks.

Lightning continued to beat down across the Russian front, large bolts fell down in droves as the red army ceased their advance and attempted to retreat. For a moment the Germans thought they were saved, the rumbling across the tundra quieted in the wake of thunder and lightning clearing across the surface. Soon the man hovered lower into the fortress and we were sure this was our end. If that…god is on the Germans side, then we were royally screwed.

A few moments later, gunfire picked up again from within the fortress, flares of light shone through slim windows and through the aiming gaps of the bunker wall. Then a giant explosion blasted through an entire section of the compound, followed by a series of smaller explosions until the base was completely aflame.

We could only stand in awe, staring across the tundra as the storm cleared over the course of some minutes. Lifeless bodies and smoking tanks, trucks, downed planes litter the snow. Spent shells and magazines thrown about, around the demolished castle sat a thick moat of smoldered cement and wood. In the distance we see Russians trying to help each other up, a fraction of the number they arrived with, limp back across the icy horizon in a terrified precession jog.

The armored god lifts from the smoky ruins of the German base, stopping again at the height he was before. His long now tattered cape bristling lightly as the winds died down. A captain of another surviving squad ordered his men to fire. I saw my men follow the command without thinking. I screamed for them to stop in a frenzied panic, I run through the men lowering their guns manually before anyone can fire. I thought I got them all when I heard a single shot from one of the sharpshooters in another squad.

Frozen, me and few other men turn slowly towards the shooter laying atop the hill overlooking our camp. He drops his gun and slides down the hill exclaiming it was a mistake, he was scared and shaking, and the trigger just went. As I move towards him to reprimand, someone from behind yells 'It's coming this way' at the top of their lungs. I turn, to see the mysterious man floating towards us slowly.

'Pick up your guns' sights up!' Another squad leader yells and everyone follows suite except me and a few other frightened individuals. As they aim a streak of lightning blast across the sky, striking through the mans torso and into the ground below. The man seemed to overload with electricity, the energy covered him completely, stalling him on his current course of action. The lightning fades and the man was gone, the crack of thunder follows suite and someone yells 'above us'.

We had an American flag posted as the rally point, without notice he' d somehow teleported through the cracks of thunder of lightning. He hovered above just thirty feet, surrounded by men aiming with guns, everyone too frozen to be the one who shoots first.

'Nobody shoot' I yelled throughout the men.

'Shoot!' Somebody else would yell.

Again, I’d yell no. Don’t. Pleading do not shoot this freaking god, you stupid hicks this man could be anything like is he even from this planet and I for one want to go home and he clearly is a virtuoso with a lightning rod. I didn’t say all that, but I thought it babe.

‘I’ve got a clear shot.’ Someone again would yell.

My response would not change. No.

Finally, the man speaks up in a calm but stern baritone voice like that of a retired teacher.

"Please. Listen to this man." Slowly, he floated down as the men cleared a circle around him, still holding up their guns as this man with brown ruffled hair and matching eyes floated to the ground.

‘What are you!’ A man from the front-line yells. ‘Yeah, You German, Russian. English? What?’ Someone else continues

As he feet touch the ground, he looks around for a second examining the men. Without catching eye contact with any one person he answers aloud.

'Well' He says. 'My dad was German, left the fatherland back in the tens. My mom, well she's a gypsy from Eastern Europe.'

'Daddy saw what was coming huh?' A soldier from my squad interjects, Blastoviz, guess he could relate to that.

'You could say that. Sadly he died on the way to New York.' The man replies.

'So you're from New York, got it. What about those powers?' Another squad leader steps up, his pistol at the ready. 'Are you friendly? Where'd you get those? Government? Whatever you are I need an explanation before I let you walk out of here.'

'What powers?' The man laughs lightly looking confused at the same time examining the shaking squad leader up and down.

'The ones you used to push back the Russians and kill them damn Jerrys in that command post? You tellin' me that wasn't you we just saw get shot down by a lightning g bolt?'

'Oh, these powers.' He opens his left hand as electricity arcs and sizzles between his fingers, wrapping across his palms like tiny structures. As we all stared mystified, behind him a slim streak of lightning shoots down and zaps the American flag at the center of the camp, exploding it from within into a billon pieces across the ice. The soldiers all snap from the trance, cocking their guns and again set sights on his head.

'Relax guys. Relax.' The man smiles still chuckling to himself, throwing his hands in the air as a show of good faith before putting them behind his back. He starts to walk through the men slowly towards the outer edge.

'Is this your home?' I speak up as he passes me, the soldiers clearing a walkway again cautiously lowering their guns. He stops for second and turns to face me.

'Not mine… I'm just the friendly next-door neighbor. Keeping house, you know, watering the plants, collecting the mail. Ensuring no one accidently knocks on any door that when opened could potentially not any threaten the very sanctity of what you call earth but also the safety of the entire universe as we know it and beyond. You know, just making sure the doors are locked and the dog gets walked.'

'What?' Is the only response I can muster up.

The man smiles before again setting off towards the edge of the men. Once he makes it a few yards from the last man he stops again before turning around to address us a final time.

'Can you guys deliver a message for me? It's not long or anything.'

'To Who?' One soldier asks, gun completely around his back.

'To everyone, everywhere. Just… just calm down, alright? Do better, please. Be, better.'

'That's vague, can you give us some specifics at least? Our superiors aren't going to treat us kindly if all we come back with is 'Calm down''. I speak up again.

The man sighs lowering his head before looking across the silent dusty tundra behind him.

'The atomic bombs they've been dropping across their deserts and across the Japanese. Look I have run-ins with the Japanese all the time, yet I've never thought about wiping them off the face of the Earth. And I could do it without all the fallout and devastating after effects of those bombs. Just tell your bosses to calm down, on the war, the violence, the bombs most of all. All that expelled energy is attracting unwanted attention from beyond your understanding, I'm doing my best to keep the peace, keep my home as well as the entirety of Earth safe. But these monstrosities, these weapons of mass destruction, too much, for the Russians, the Germans, Americans. All animals the same, the wolf, the jackal, and the vulture.' He pauses as he begins to lift carelessly from the ground. About ten feet above he looks down at us once more before darting away.

'While a part of me still believes that fate is an unwritten play, I have seen the worse and best of all futures ahead for our shared world. I cannot say this in a more serious fashion." He crosses his arms as he again begins to float away slow at first before blasting off at the haste and speed of a shooting star over the horizon towards where we landed. His last words before ascending through the clouds, 'Do better'.

The squads moving again. We're maybe less than a day's trek from the ships, docked on the shore. I better go, we took a few casualties, so everyone has to pull extra weight if we expect to keep pace and momentum you know. I'll write you when we dock in Hawaii, love you Karalyn. Damn I miss you. You don't even know.

Chapter 6

The Testimony of the Second Solidius

This is my final testimony, my final account of all I have seen since the voices of the Lightning Lake convinced me to leave Earth and the returning reign of the beacon continent Mu. My home realm of Earth, now such a distant memory, was beautiful in its prime. Once I sat ruler of a mystical land, shining brighter than any where else on Earth. For centuries, an ancient power sat beneath a lost continent. My father discovered this power, losing himself basking in the awe if his discovery. I was pulled from life in another land and brought to this island and drank from the mystical lake he'd built a society on.

After his death I spent years training myself, building up his legacy and the county he'd started with the help a few loved ones. Soon I had children of my own, a boy, hot-headed, short-tempered, always lost, always wandering, always curious. I was for sure he'd be an explorer when he got older. I didn't want to pass the Island on, I'd realized the people wanted elections and I had to give it to them eventually.

For years now, I'd been having terrible dreams of shadow people following me, chasing me, watching me as I sleep. I wonder if this is connected to the political state of the island corrupting my psyche. My daughter brought me solace in times of unperilled stress, she talks me through my dreams as we sit for tea in the garden each morning before she'd sets off to school.

I also had a daughter, conceived and born in the very lake from which I and the island itself drew its power. Alice, she was an angel. More confident then I was at her age, smarter. She wanted the crown, she had plans for the direction of the country as well the world, all in a positive direction. She was about progression and family. Her brother on the other hand, selfish, destructive, irresponsible. He succumbs bed to many addictions throughout my time with him.

It soon became clear he wanted the same throne as his sister. Knowing what he'd do with that power, I set out to denounce our royalty and give in to the fight for free elections. My family would retain their ownership of the lake and all its attributes, so long as we kept pumping it into hospitals and power plants. Anything for the security of my people, anything to put them better at ease. One night I was stricken with a terrible nightmare wherein I found myself drowning in the very lake used to empower.

The voices of the lake told me it was time to leave. These same voices taught me how to utilize its power, they sat quietly as my father, and so many others died in my arms long before. It'd been a while since they directly spoke to me, they once told me we would have to have a talk, I didn't think he'd be like this. Upon waking in a cold sweat, I rushed to the lake to take a dip. Get connected with the forces and reach them somehow and get more understanding on what that dream meant.

As I lay in the waters, again they embrace me, taking control over my entire being and my vision fades to white. Again, they tell me, its time to leave. I'd come to a level beyond any Earthbound Lightbringer before me. It was time for a new duty station. See there's this door beneath the ice continent of Antarctica. Long ago the original Lightbringer defeated an ancient galaxy eater, both beings were destroyed. The bringer bled, an island of incomparable beauty emerged. The creature of darkness bled, portals sizzle open and a flood of demon's spring through, burning forests, devouring animals whole, blackening seas.

The voices showed me the second bringer, who pushed back the hordes of demons, closing the portals by burying the giant beasts severed tongue, still wiggling profusely as he dug beneath the continent of Antarctica, the only debris from the fight fully intact. Most of the monster was destroyed in the fight with the original, its pieces flung through space. I'd protected the land above as the bringers before me did. Perhaps my family reached too far outside our jurisdiction a few times, but with great power, I mean come on, you must take responsibility, right?

Anyway, I knew all this. What I didn't know what that I wasn't the only piece of the bringer in the universe, he was blast about just as the monster was and that thing under the ice wasn't the only piece of that ancient evil either. The creature was reassembling, soon, what was already assembled would come to earth for his tongue, destroying it as he came. The voices tell me his tongue has been talking to humans over the centuries, inspiring wickedness and evil all the like. The voices tell me my son hears this dark tongue, and because of this intertwined evil, his future remains unclear. Thus, creating an unclear future for Sunlatveria as it once was.

They tell me its on me, find the other pieces of the bringer, and intercept the being before it makes it to the Andromeda galaxy. The connection between the beast and its pieces would rip the tongue from the planet, kicking off the end of days for all humanity. It wouldn't even be days, the Earth would be ripped apart, its inhabitants tossed into the vaccum of space. Earth, all its history and potential, destroyed just like that. After they broke it down for me, I couldn't say no. I couldn't refuse. I thought of my children, my life, my island.

Up until this point, I wasn't fused with the lake fully. Id have to take a bath whenever I needed my powers really. Sure, Ali and Alice were different, but they were born in the lake, I was a mere human compared to these demigods. The voices then added to their original proposal.

'You set off with this mission as your goal, we will never leave you.'

I'd fuse with the lake a hundred percent. As long as there would be enough energy left in the lakes reservoir to power the island for a few more years I was happy. One downfall of this only mentioned when it was too late, because of me, the spirits would leave the pools, forever bonded with I as we trek across the universe to gather ourselves up to full strength. For this I worry, for what happens when my misguided son uses the lake, no one will be there to teach him as I had the voices as well as Edwin.

'You mustn't dwell on this.' The voices remind me as I begin for a final bath, one that would see me off to the other side of the cosmos for god knows how long. I say a final goodbye to my children and my children only. Alice, still so young, will hardly remember much of me, will she even recognize this as a goodbye? I wonder. Will Rex bend my goodbye to fit his childish agenda?

I couldn't dwell on this. Enough pieces of the beast had reunited where I could feel his tug on my planet. I could hear his words in the background of the wind on a stormy night. I had to leave.

Before this I'd only seen the cosmos through visions, unclear dreams of odd symmetry and color. I'd find myself floating amount brightly lit star systems and beautifully crafted nebulas of gas and rock. I spent what seemed like years sleeping in the lowest crevices of the lakes massive tunneling system. Fusing with the ancient forces, molecule by molecule, atom by atom, cell by cell it took over my being. My consciousness was still there, mu physical appearance. But I was no longer human beneath the skin, I could feel a constant stream of energy moving around me, through me. I was connected. I could feel the other side of the Earth, the other side of the moon, everything was connected in the ether.

'A bringer has been struck down on the other side of the cosmos, on its own this being attempted to delay the great gathering. For this he failed, and the deadline as moved up as the beast had gained a substantial amount of energy from this encounter. It's time to move, you have depleted this source of our divinity, leave your people this reservoir, its energy, with proper, management can still power your home for half a millennium. We must gather the remaining fractions of light before the darkness beyond can consume them.'

So, we began. I expected to wake in the tunnels as I did decades ago. But no, I awoke in full armor, floating alone aimlessly just beyond the moon. The Earth shrinking faster and faster as I involuntarily list further away at increasing speeds. I soon found myself in a completely new system of planets, each more unrecognizable than the last. We travelled vast distance is what seemed like mere hours, soon we came to the first stop on our journey. A lifeless scarred planet with a sun and moon similar to my own. A giant storm of wind and lightning whipped across the planet's surface and the voices spoke again for the first time since we'd left my home.

'Billions once called this place home... our power corrupted the soil. Corrupted their morality and decimated their sciences. They could not hear out voices clearly through the fog of distrust and paranoia they'd created among themselves.' I look around the ruins of the dead planet, desolate dunes of sand stretch as far as I can see.

'I can't even tell someone lived here, are we too late.' I speak up over the dusty low breeze picking up.

'We are too late to save the species that once inhabited this plain. But we have arrived just in time to regain a portion of our magnificence.'

'What do you m...' Before I finish I feel the wind pick up harder, I turn to see the massive storm I'd seen from space pouring over the horizon.

I knew what I had to do, or more realistically, the voices granted me the wisdom to see my objective clearly. Inside the heart of storm, shining brightly through the deadly winds and heavy crystal rain, spun a slim tornado of shining white winds similar to the special way the lightning of us would glow.

'Into the eye Harry.' Without hesitation I lock my arms to the side as I shoot off the ground skyward, curving towards the beastly storm approaching closer and closer.

'Shield me!' I scream subconsciously as I break through the most outer layer of the storm wall. The winds stringer than I'd anticipated, the bits of shining rock rain small at first, harmless, soon shift into boulders and slabs of stone being hurled at speeds over Mach four, the shield reflects some, other too big to bounce push me back instead. I soon find myself again on the ground atop a rocky landscape, my vision obscured from the thick unearthly hurricane beating down above. I readied myself for another risky leap into the heart of the monster when the voices spoke again.

'Don't jump.' I paused, relaxing my stance. "Wait for your moment Harry.'

I obeyed. If I haven't mentioned how disturbing it is to hear my dead little sisters nickname for me said by the distorted overlapping voices of a thousand past bringers, its quite startling each time. Nevertheless, I obeyed and waited. Standing with my legs parted and hands clasped behind my back. Visibility was low, so I opted to just close my eyes until something spoke to me again. And it did, not the voices as I expected. But I felt a drop in the wind, the rise in temperature. My eyes shoot open and without thought or deliberation I blasted from the surface into what was the eye of the storm.

No lethal wind or rain, for a moment there was nothing inside the cyclone, then the heavenly twister descends from the upper clouds, decimating the rock formations blow as it touches ground. I hover in place with my arms at the ready as it approaches me slowly.

'UTU, ANNA, UTU ANA!' The voices repeat oddly over and over again as the whirlwind makes contact with my hands extended out on front of me. I feel a sudden urge to grab the twister and toss its unnatural existence into the sun. Something inside me resisting the temptations of power and wisdom offered by the voices of Old. I ignore my gut, my instinct of mistrust and caution and in doing so I give in, turning my self over to the ancient spirits of fundamental nature.

There is no vision or reaction once the tornado devours me, for a moment I find myself inside the beast surrounded by light so intense my eyes strained to stay open. The cyclone dissipated, as did the entire storm circling about. Silence and calmness fell across the once raging planet and the voice spoke again in its normal disturbing tone.

'To the next Harry, soon we will be able to prevent the great gathering and the close the gates of oblivion for good. Finish what we started so long ago my brother.'

I swear through the distortion I hear Abigails soft cry hidden beneath the thousands and it frightens me to obey without question and again I find myself drifting towards an unknown destination beyond the stars that lie.

Chapter 7

Shots in the dark

"Avery? Travis Ellis Avery?" An older dark-skinned woman with slim hips and thick legs come from behind an office door. I stand up, following her into the small seven by seven room without a view. The walls covered with various maps, certifications and acknowledgements.

"Take a seat Mr. Woodard, my name is Eleanor Avery you can call me El for the duration of this meeting, alright sweetheart?" I take my seat nodding profusely, locking my fingers in my lap as I settle into the unexpected soft cushions.

"So the form here says..." She scans a folder of documents before I speak up.

"I-I'm trying to get granted a work visa, destination is South Africa." The woman is still silently reading the paperwork.

"You've got family there huh, already got work lined up?" She continues. "Wait, I see it right here." She flips a page. "Seems you've got all your paperwork in order Mr. Woodard, let me just push it through and you should receive your passport and the rest of your necessary documents within forty-eight hours. If you want them faster, you can come back tomorrow morning and we'll have everything waiting for you."

"Thank you so much ma'am, if you don't mind I'll be here in the morning to pick those up." I rise from the chair smiling gleefully as she shakes my hand reaffirming.

"You're lucky, not a lot of people are getting visas these days with the protests and more than eighty percent of the national defense away."

"How'd I get approved then? Was it my good looks and silent charm?" I laugh kind of awkwardly and she joins in smiling lightly.

"Someone must be looking out for ya. Come back tomorrow morning to pick up your travel documents, they should be ready around 11." She takes a seat waving me out before picking up another folder to browse through.

"Well… thanks!" I make my way outside and to the parking lot, a friend from work had driving me to the application office, he sat atop the hood of his car downing cigarette after cigarette until I'd returned.

"Finally! I thought I was gonna die of lung cancer before you got out of there." He hops of the car and enters the drivers seat as I enter the passenger side.

"Relax Luka, it was barely twenty minutes." I say putting on my seatbelt.

"Did everything go through? Are you good?" He looks over after he starts up the vehicle and heads out of the parking structure.

"Yeah, well I still have come back tomorrow to pick up everything, but I can go, after all the run around I can finally get outta here."

"I still don't think you should go man, Jenny needs you and Molly says they need people at the Gear factory so come on down. Nakito motors takes diligent care of its people I've heard and you've been living in the fringe too long it's time to get a job." The car turns into traffic. "Am I taking you back to your Jennys place or yours, are you still living in the Rehab Ward on fortieth, what's up?"

"I can't just stay at your place? It's one night! I pick up my paperwork at eleven tomorrow, the ship leaves at four I'll be outta your hair before the wife even notices."

"I'm sorry but she will notice you my friend, last day in town or not. I'm taking you to Jennys. Say goodbye before you ditch town for good, have you even told her yet?"

"No, she loves it here. Besides I don't need to drag her into my mess. I've been out on parole for three weeks. We've had a nice ride in that short time but I aint attached. All I want to do is put this island in the rearview and never look back."

"But hasn't she been down in Kobain protesting the war? She still wants to stay here despite her distain for the administration and its tentacles as she calls them."

"In her head this place will always be the land of the enlightened like they taught us in high school and elementary. Her home where she grew up, raised her kids her parents grew up here and their parents so on. Me personally, I've always had a funny feeling about this place."

"Then why'd you join the military so quick? I mean you must've saw something in the green, white and black that filled you with hope." Luka laughs lightly as he turns onto a speedway.

"Ya know, you know an awful lot about me for a bartender I met a few weeks ago."

"Come one Travis, you're in my tavern every night, you're there til its empty. You helped me clear those vested kids from the parking lot that one night. I'm gonna miss ya when ya leave man, I've never had such a loyal customer. I wish I was enough to keep ya here." He jokes, swerving in and out of lanes.

"Ah well, anyway... what were we talking about?"

"You've been thinking about this huh? You've never talked about why you left the military or why you went to prison. I imagine whatever you saw or did sent your view of the country askew. We'll if it helps you feel better, they kinda always deserved it right? I mean America. I mean, for years their media and administrations mocked us as their industries slowly began to rely on us. We did nothing but give to the word, countless, unlimited resources without scarring the Earth, they should've praised us, thanked us daily on every news channel. No to mention the additional advancements in science and medicine that were made here my friend. Here, not in England or Germany. For the last two centuries we have been the almighty, giver of life and knowledge. We did nothing to provoke their invasion which was followed by an intercontinental ballistic missile might I remind you. They deserved Hawaii. They deserved California."

"Didn't realize how patriotic you were Luka, we?" I ask raising an eyebrow."

"You know what I meant. Look I'm sorry for showing some pride in my homeland. I was born here; four generations of my family were born here. I'm glad he's out there defending us, protecting us. The American homeland invasion might be going on for longer than it needed, but I mean they basically have the West coast completely rebuilt so there's a plus."

"Luke they're shooting children in the street, bombing hospitals, dropping radiation shells on top of shelters. The war isn't over just because they've put the Americans into a corner. Rebellion brews across the world, all empires fall."

"Where are you getting this? The occupation has been going on for over eighty years now and I've yet to hear anything so graphic hit the airways. Nothing like that sits in the history books we were forced to read in school."

"Forced. You said forced. Let's just say I didn't go to prison because I did something wrong, I went to prison because I saw something I wasn't supposed to. Nothing showing Sunlatveria in a negative light as ever hit the airways, even international channels. The only outspoken country was America for decades upon decades. It's a singularity, Sunlatveria has become the new, center, the new beacon of mankind. The SNG (Sunlatverian National Government) is following the same guide as twentieth century America did, but quicker, quieter, deadly. This is the new Rome." The car stops in front of a familiar apartment building, Jennys'. The sky is dark now, her block filled with people.

"Look man I have to get back to the tavern. Zur can only manage it for so long without me., I'll be able to give you a ride to your transport though, which ship is it?"

"The Chula Vista, dock M ten."

"And once you land in Johannesburg you're not coming back huh?" He says offputtingly as he puts the car in park for a moment.

"Listen to me man..." I sigh unbuckling the seat harness. "I know you love this place, you'd die for it. But somethings been calling me, from beyond the shores of Converse and Hera, for years I've ignored it and did what I was taught to believe was right. I can't ignore it any longer, it's like a shadow, telling me to run." Luka laughs again before waving me out, pressing a button that opens that door automatically forcing me to go.

"I don't understand Travis, but as your only friend, I support you, hey have a good night man. I'll call you tomorrow when I get to the office." I step out, slamming the door shut behind me.

"Alright man, drive safe." He starts to pull away slowly. "Have a good night!" I yell once more before he gets too far, and I turn towards the building and process inside, hurrying up the stairs.

Loud electronic dance music can be heard pumping throughout her entire for, seeping from her door along with shafts of colored lights illuminating the cracks of the door. Another reason I needed to leave, I walk in the door of her apartment to see her on the floor hunched over her glass coffee table cutting lines in some glassy powder with a switchblade. The apartment was full of people I didn't recognize, wall to wall tweakers and randoms smoking and dancing about. Through the clouded and packed hallway, I go, the music deafening as the sound echoes through my chest with each beat.

"What's going here!?" I scream to Jenny as I struggle to get through the crowd.

"Travis?! What are you doing here?!" She looks up yelling from the table. I can barely hear her through the noise. I take her hand and drag her to her bedroom, kicking out a group of people already going at it on her bed, slamming the door behind them.

"You don't have to be so rude Travis damn." She rolls her eyes as she plops on the bed near her nightstand and pulling out a pre-rolled cigarette and a small box of matches. She lights her cigarette and tosses the match into nearby metallic trash bin near the door.

"Jenny what the hell is going on here? What are you doing cutting powder out there huh?! You've been clean almost two years, why are you throwing that in the trash? And who are all these people?"

Taking a slow drag from her cigarette, she crosses her arms before answering.

"First of all, that's some new lightning infused ice, all of the high, none of the side effects. Made from the finest shards hand-picked from the lightning caverns, it really does even more than that like-" Derailing her, I interject.

"I don't give a shit about the drugs, tell me why, why you are doing this. Where are your kids." I sigh, silently thinking about how a few days ago she was doing so good. Working, in school, clean, healthy. I was sure I was free to leave, and I was leaving no one in bad shape, all she has is me so how could I leave now.

"The big one has the little one and the middle ones at a friends for the night. Iman saw you at the passport office yesterday, and then again this morning. Care to tell me where you're going?" She questions looking up at me more serious now. I sigh again before rubbing my head down to my chin.

"I'm going to Africa okay... but what does that have to do with all these god damn people here and with you shoveling glass up your nose?"

"Because Travis what's the damn point!? You're not going to be here, I have to start making new friends sometime." She stands in a huff and rushes outside back to her party.

"Wow." I say aloud to myself, almost ready to completely bail.

I catch up to here on the balcony of the living room, on the eighth floor her view looked over the Volstagg woods, the moon shining bright above the horizon so magnificently.

She tries to short some powder off a tray, but I manage to smack the entire tray over the ledge before she can get a taste.

"What the hell Travis, that shit wasn't cheap you bitch!" She crosses her arms aggressively and turns towards the ledge and the view. I wrap my arms around her waist from behind, softly kissing her head through her thicket of brown locks.

"Don't touch me." She says brushing me off, barely looking up. "Not until you tell me why you're leaving me." Still pecking her head lightly, I reply softly.

"It's not you for one alright. First of all we've only been together a few weeks, I don't understand why you're so attached." She pushes away for a second but I hold her tight laughing it off kissing her again. Despite the shirt time, I was quite attached, moreso than Id ever been to anyone.

"I just see... I feel something terrible coming, something terrible happening already. I need to break from the Sunlatverian surveillance network, I need unbiased news about the world. I want that information without getting flagged either. With my criminal record, there's a celling here I can't punch through, I got my passport approved through sheer luck." She turns in a fuss.

"So, what? You can't just abandon me, your people, you fought and bled for them you deserve to have your peace here. This is home, we've been here since birth, our parents have been here since birth. Come with me to this rally tomorrow, we're driving to Solitude to protests outside the main palace gates. Do you really think you're the only one here that's trying to find out what else is happening in the world? We've been pushing free press and less control for years, ugh, I told you all this several times already, you never fucking listen and even if you do is not as important as the other misfit shit you got rattling around in your head so it's just in one ear and out the other with you!" She storms back into the party still rambling obscenities loudly and out the front door, I stay in hot pursuit.

I finally catch up to her outside the building sitting on the front step, slumped over her knees staring at a dark derelict building across the street. Silently I drop down beside her, sitting on my hands as a night breeze rolled pass.

"That building over there used to be a wine distillery or something like that." She speaks up over her knees bent up. "You can see the old vineyard sketching behind it, its so unkept these days."

"And the one next to it?"

"The islands first Oceanology Society Museum.

"Like the big glass one downtown?" She laughs lightly hearing the question.

"All the buildings have glass. But yeah, they moved there after there was an incident in here in 2088, some junkie broke in and died trying to swim down to the lightning veins." She extracts another cigarette from her pants pocket. "Shit I don't have a lighter." She stands up and looks around when she spots a group of building loitering in the empty lot next to the abandoned museum. The group of four or five young adults danced around a garbage can fire while David Bowie blasted loudly from a speaker hidden in a backpack on the ground near the can. "Come on." Jenny commands as she heads across the street pulling my hand. Beyond the empty lot I see another man hidden in the bushes watching the teenagers, shrouded completely in shadow and darkness, no feature poked through other than that he was of average height. I turned to examine to rest of the street, coming back to his bush, he was gone.

"You know they pulled those shards from beneath this building here, this guy Charles, also known as big time dealer Ceelos. This guy drained the water in the tunnels and started mining the crystal buildup, lace any drug with this stuff, multiply your high by a million and subtract all the harmful side effects. Crazy shit yeah?" She explains unaware of the eerie watcher, wrapping her arm around mine as we approach one of the teens with a lit cigarette. She gets a light to hers from his and they exchange a brief hello and thank you. She starts to question the kid and what they were doing out here and then she invites them upstairs to her loft on the eighth floor. They all agree and soon we all begin to head upstairs together.

With one foot in the street and the other in the gutter, I stop for a moment when I feel a cold shiver creep up from behind. I turn towards the building and for a split second a see a man shaped shadow in the window on the first floor, only a few yards away, it disappears in a blink, I question my sanity for a second.

"What are you doing Trav come on." Jenny tries to pull me, the others already in her apartment building.

"I thought I saw-" A loud squeal from within the decaying gallery interrupts me. Jenny steps begins to move towards the boarded front entrance. "Sounds like a kid, come on let's see what's up."

"A kid, sounds more like a pig getting slaughtered." I step towards her grabbing her shoulders as she attempts to pry open the boarding. "Jenny it's my last night here okay, I don't want to spend it exploring some dusty, spooky old manor."

"Travis…" She kicks through a final hedge effectively clearing a route in, down he long hallway I see the shadow man again at the very end, poking out of a door way before disappearing again in a blink. "Someone's in trouble, police won't get in time. Let's go."

Hesitate I follow, but not before pulling my phone from my jacket and sending a medical alert message to the local police department. I stay silent on the appearing of the shadow creature, I would deny his existence for as long as it remained harmless.

Jenny picks up a thick piece of pipe laying on the ground near the entrance and silently moves down the creaky hallway, checking each corner with the light of her handheld as she went. I follow, my device shining as well hanging from a chest pocked on my jacket, so I could grip whatever blunt object I'd find with both hands. We come to the door where the shadow stood, it led to a small hallway with some stairs leading down to the basement presumably. Its here I find a large rusting pipe wrench for defense and we here hear scream again. It echoes from further below, without words Jenny continues, waving me to follow as with each creaking step she creeps down the dark and cob webbed stairs.

We finally come to a cold stone cellar with soaring high ceilings and shelves stacked high with barrels and crates. In the back of the room through the rows of shelving, blue and white lights shine through from an unknown source. Before we can continue, a gunshot echoes through the cellar and at the same shoulder shuddering moment, I'm grabbed by an unknown man by the back of the collar.

"What the hell are you doing down here?!" The man says in a scarred and heavy voice. Turning I see a man in a black button up with black slacks on holding a gun towards the back of Jennys head. Two more men come from behind him as he lowers the gun.

"What's going on over there?" Another voice calls from the back corner of the room where the light was shining from. One man grabs Jenny by the shoulders and another drags me, and we move towards the back as a man casually steps out with his hand clasped behind him, two more men step out from the corner, each silent thug carrying large unnecessary pistols at the ready.

"Jenny? What the hell are you doing down here?" In a smooth and calming familiar voice a man replied from the shadows near the glowing illumination. The man steps closer and moves his hands to his front, holding a small knife, his hands and the blade both covered in blood. His face comes into view, Ceelos, also known as Charles or Chuck Dagger as I knew him. I'd served with him decades ago in a Marine Infiltration unit over in the America during the Midwestern Push.

"I heard someone screaming, thought someone was in danger." She wriggles free from the man holding her, and the room relaxes a little more.

"Someone was in danger, but Its over now." He tosses the knife to one of his subordinates as another tosses him a clean white rag. "Tell me Jennifer, who's your friend here?" He points to me as he cleans his hands slowly.

"This is my-" She starts but I interject.

"I'm Ellis, Travis Ellis. Look I don't care about your little crystal operation here, I'm leaving town tomorrow I don't need any trouble or any of this unnecessary bullshit." I'd been holding my hands up since I first saw the gun, I was finally feeling comfortable to put them down, luckily, he didn't remember my face, last I saw him was in New Mexico. We were taking part in a series of raid along the border wall established to hunt down and eliminate the remaining cartels that existed in the area. Mexico gave us clearance to do what the hell we wanted. He disappeared during one of these raids and was assumed dead.

"Yeah Ceelos, I'm sorry, we weren't trying to pry or anything, I didn't even consider that it could've been you or your guys down here. I heard a scream and just started running towards it."

Ceelos laughs stepping turning towards the mysterious light shining form the back corner.

"Never pegged you for the hero type Jenny. Coming to me for all that crystal the other day, boy didn't expect this from you." The thugs push us to follow around the corner, revealing a large hole in the corner, light shining brightly from within.

"Come take a look you two." He waives us over, before I have a chance to think the black shirted older man behind me pushes me forward again. We come to edge where Ceelos stand, blood splatter painted one slab of the holes edge. I peer over the edge cautiously, the tunnel walls dotted with large and small crystal shards. A line of blood dripped down forming a stripe of red contrasting against the blue and white shimmering.

"No need to scare us Ceelos, we didn't see anything. We don't know anything." Jenny goes on, I knew she feared heights and now so did Ceelos as she began to shake harder as the man pushed us closer.

"Sorry Jennifer, I don't take chances, I don't like risks. I'm not one for luck, or intervening gods or *maybe* this person will do right by me and keep their damn mouth shut. Never works out like that, spent too many years locked up thinking on small mistakes. I'm engineering something wonderful, something beyond drugs and money. I'm talking about a future, not just for me. For every one of my people too. We're going to take this island and reform it."

"Boss, this guy sent a medical alert before he came in. The message was intercepted by our plug in the PD and he shot it over to me. They'll be here any minute." The thug behind me who'd originally caught us exclaimed.

"This spot is burned boss, we have to get you over to West Sol. They can't find you, the whole operation would be halted, luckily we got all the equipment out this morning." The guard behind Jenny says.

"That wasn't luck that was me being on top of shit while you guys just lounge about doing god knows what?!" The mad leader screams at the man before turning back in between Jenny and I, whispering softly

"I'm the only one..." He chuckles lightly. "In the public sector at least, who's figured out how to manipulate these crystals. See the government wants me dead for this, Solidius has a personal death squad, have you heard of them? The Entropy Committee? *Sooooo* deadly, *soooo* mysterious. They have ways of getting intel and information beyond all realms of possible warfare." He laughs louder and heavier, hissing with his tongue, whispering a final time before heading off. "I won't let them find me."

We turn towards the guards as Ceelos disappears around a corner with the three guards that brought us here, leaving us with the two that'd been here prior.

"Kill them!" Ceelos yells from upstairs somewhere and the two men raise their guns aiming. Jenny throws her hands up as does I, both screaming ,No, over and over again hoping somehow that'd work. The one on front of me lets off a shot and it hits me in the shoulder, I stumble, falling into the pit. In a matter of seconds, my head smashes against the wall, flipping me. I hear another gunshot from above just before I hit a collection of crystal head on and I'm knocked unconscious.

A thud against me jolts me awake. A flood of rush washes over me throughout my entire body, blood dripping form cuts of my faces, neck and hands. I call to Jenny, her head draped over my stomach oddly. My body presses up against another unfamiliar lifeless body, the shining gems provided some light in the worm-like cave. It twisted further down, we'd landed on some bending in the tunneling. I call her again, no response so slowly I move her off me and I see it. She'd taken her shot in the head. I check the other body, the one that brought us here. A young boy, his face cut up just as mine was from the fall but worse from Ceelos playing with him with his knife; lifeless, he lay with another shot in the head. He must've come across that paranoid warlords operation by accident just as we did.

I sit up to lean against the cave wall when I notice my left leg twisted, the bone snapped in half, plucking a cigarette from Jennys pocket. I remembered she didn't have a lighter, luckily, I'd grabbed hers from the loft upstairs before we'd left in a futile attempt to stall her from smoking. I began taking drags from it when down the other end of the tunnel where the decline started up again, the shadow creature watching.

Silently, I continue taking drags, watching him as he watches me.

"You fucking bitch. I'm dead alright, come kill me or leave to fuck alone to die in relative peace!" I scream at the monster, astonishingly enough, it obeys, disappearing again in the darkness. I take a few easy breaths, blood from the cluster of bodies pooling around me, the crystals beneath shimmering brightly as the thick dark carpet expanded.

The shadow again appears, this time closer, standing with its head cocked as the cave had a low ceiling. From its direction I could hear a low static, steadily increasing in volume. I looked around for something to defend myself when I remembered some relevant information from school concerning these crystals and these caverns. Harold the Second Solidius, used to stab himself with shards of lightning glass, granted him enough strength and agility to hunt badgerboars and scorpionmoths unarmed. It's the same energy Ceelos is experimenting with, the same shit Jenny was smoking, the same ancient energy that had been powering our humble abode for centuries.

"Eat." A familiar voice rings from down the tunnel behind the figure. "Eat, eat, eat!" It says again, cutting clearly through the rising static. The gems and shards lining the walls begin pulsating lightly as the shadow disappeared and reemerged again closer, now he stood less than ten feet away. A large shard the length and thickness of a banana falls into my lap, presumably braking off from the ceiling from the lively glowing.

I pick up the shard and it shocks me, I drop it in the puddle of blood between my thighs. I pick it up again, it continues to shock me, I grind my teeth accepting the pain as some karmic punishment. In front of me the shadow vanishes again before reemerging directly in front of me, its face extended to face me only inches away and it spoke in what sounded like a muffled rapture of a million overlapping souls.

"Why die?" It asked slowly before disappearing again, this time leaving behind a cloud of jet black smoke, it rises, dissipating across the jagged ceiling. The white noise vanishes as well, leaving me again to contemplate death all alone. Confused and hesitate, I examine the shards around me for a moment, wiping the blood away with the only clean area of my shirt.

"Harold used to stab himself with the shards if I remember correctly."

I question this aloud for a moment, before accepting it and grabbing the best-looking piece I could find. I grab one and hold it ready above an exposed piece of my leg. With a mighty howl, I plunge the shard of crystal about seven inches long into my right thigh, my pants torn from the fall. The pain was brief, I'd been stabbed before, but I wasn't expecting the shock of half a million volts that sends me backwards. I knock my head against the craggy cave wall and all goes dark for a moment.

I awake a few moments later in the same spot, blood disappeared from my face and leg. Jenny still dead as well as the other nameless corpse who'd drug us here. The main in my leg and shoulder were gone, as well as the face and throat pain. I felt completely fine, able to stand even so I do. My leg was heled, back in place. I could breathe normally again, my heart rate was calm. I spit an out a tiny fragment of colorless dim crystal, bloody, onto the ground before whipping my mouth with my shirt. As I stretched my legs and arms, a rush of energy and power swims through my entire being. I'd spent a lot of time on the wrong side of the law, but I really hadn't touched many drugs like that before. This felt more amazing than what I'd expect any drug to feel.

I felt confident that I could climb from the cave I'd been thrown down. I began climbing up the sides when I feel an urge to leap upward, I do, kicking off a stash of crystals from the wall as I do but I find myself at least thirty yards higher than I was. After a few times I was out of the cave and again standing in the dark stone cellar.

Another one of Ceelos hired help, stands over a crate in a corner opposite the pit, packing some last-minute items someone must've forgot about. The man talks into his handheld pressed up against his head with his shoulder to free up his hands.

"They just arrived actually, they're probably about to begin searching the upper levels then they'll be down here so I need to-"

"Forget it, we have forty-nine other properties across the island. Nothing here will blow us. Go, now." A familiar voice on the phone yells.

"Yes boss." The phone call ends and he put the device away, closing the crate before pulling out his pistol and begins screwing on a suppressor.

"Is that for the police?" I ask brazenly.

"What the-?" He turns around shocked and begins firing wilding in my direction. I felt confidence I'd never felt, but nothing in me told me I'd be okay against bullets.

Without flinching. I take a few shots to the gut as I charge towards the man with my hands up. Beneath my skin, my veins glowing a bright blue tinted white. Id recognized the glow from old text book photos of Queen Ali and her savage defense of the Corinthian and the Mountains of Ra. The bullets meant nothing, for I was protected. I grab the mans throat with both hands and in a second, I realize my newfound powers. I squeeze with the force of a small child and his necks snaps like celery. His body slumps to the floor and the room falls silent as the struggles die with him.

Sirens blare closer and closer in the distance. My senses heightened, my brain unmuddied by random thoughts and distraction, I hear police breaching the derelict apartment building above and make a snap decision to head back into the tunnels. If I wanted Ceelos, I'd find him near his source of income and the tunnels would connect each possible location mentioned before by the guard.

I slide down the tunnel wall as hastily as possible and I soon find myself in the same bend as before. Surprisingly, the two bodies that occupied this space with me before had disappeared, leaving behind only a bloodied spot on the ground and a fading trail leading down the other end of the tunnel. The darkness is thick, this area had a high concentration of special light crystals that did not extend down the tunnel. Luckily my veins were still glowing brightly and even begun pulsating since being back in the tunnel. By concentrating I could intensifying the brightness or bring it down, I went to the maximum setting and started towards the darkness. My illuminating bloodstream provided me with little comfort as it lit none of the path in front of me past a foot, so I had to think of something else.

I extended a hand out into the cold, my eyes closed I began to focus on light, creating it, willing it to me. A warm feeling enveloped my hand, I fling open my eyes to find I hand created a light source in my extended hand. An extremely bright light illuminating every crevice of the tunnel before and behind me, it was stunning, beautiful. Just beyond the miracle I'd just manifested stood a rat-faced behemoth of wet black spikey patched fur, lurching over because it was too big for the tunnel. Its giant rat paws up and at the attack, without screaming I jump back in fright, the light dispels as the beast surges forward bursting from the darkness.

It swipes at my legs and I fall backwards, slamming against the rock as it scrambles to get on top of me. It screeches loudly as I began kicking to get it off, liters of saliva dripping from its gaping mouth trying to bite my head off. The veins begin to intensify, and smoke begins to rise form where the beast contacts me. Its skin sizzles and it screeches louder rearing for a moment that I use to break free from its domination. I ball a first and channel as much power and focus as I can into my right hand and fly at the creature with the hook ready. I follow the punch, heavier than a car, as it sends the creature smashing into the wall. It howls as it tries to stand back up on its hid and front legs before falling over again continuing to whimper.

I step towards the wounded monster and do the same focus technique on my right foot as I stomp down just below his watering deformed eye. The whimpers cut off and I'm again left in the stillness. Stepping over the beast slumped up again the tightening cave walls, I press onward into the tunnels, positive I'd avenged at least one of my former lovers' killers and confident I'd be able to handle whatever I happen to come across.

I come to a downward bend into more darkness. Without hesitation, I slide down the walls and continue forward, I let nothing stop me. Now in a protected state of being, I march on as time passes. One thing on my mind, revenge, the thought warms me. Hours pass it seems, through bends and twists and turn I follow the tunnels. Passing giant crystal caverns and beautiful underground rivers of pure light. In one of the less grander tunnels, I discovered a path again full of light crystals that's I began to follow despite how tight and small the journey grew. I soon found myself sneaking up on some armed guards and workers huddled around a shining small hole in the ground, the glow shadowed the room full of crystals that surrounded it.

A tunnel in the back of the chamber ascended to the surface, it was the only entrance to the room beside the path I'd shimmied through. The room is littered with machinery and tubing, after a few moments of stalking, Ceelos arrives accompanied by a small platoon of more men at the ready with large caliber machine guns.

"Over here sir!" One of the men near the mysterious hole yells over to the approaching Ceelos, hands behind his back, his curly hair bouncing as he walks.

"Have we found it?" Ceelos speaks up still a few yards away as the ground around the hole yield to give him a full view and I see the splashing of the light river from earlier. I think back to school and everything we learned about the light rivers, how it made the Second a god, how it created the great Queen Ali and her daughter Princess Alice of Solitude. How it drove the rest of the Hebranks crazy, lead them to suicide, exile or worse.

The group continues talking, discussing their miraculous find but I couldn't hear a thing, so I try to maneuver a little bit closer, keeping hidden in the darkness behind several downed stalactites. A guard spots me and yells for the others to fire, they commence their firing squad as I remain ducked behind the rocks and jagged stalagmites.

"Stop! Stop! Stop!" Ceelos yells as the gunfire fades. "Guys this a perfect opportunity. I was going to test my new powers out on one of you, instead Ill just test them on our little intruder here. Someone, quick, bring him over here."

I Look down at my skin preparing to attack when I notice the glow is almost gone, on top of that Id taken a bullet in my left shoulder before I hit the ground and it was starting to sting, the blood wasn't disappearing and began to drench my clothes as I gripped it. Soon I found myself surrounded my three goons, unarmed they grab me by my arms and legs and drag me over just yards from the hole. I clenched my teeth trying to hold in the pain, their man-handling would've dislocated both arms had I been completely drained of the power.

"Oh, wow it's you... You survived, somehow." Ceelos looks down at me, checking both sides of my face with his white alligator shoes. He takes a step back to address the room. "How ignorant of you. You must've had the power right in front of you, but you nothing of its ways or of it secrets." He continues before turning to his men extending his arms to his sides.

"This is a lesson on two fronts. One, I need to start makin' sure you fucks are really doing your fucking jobs." The men in the room tighten up fearing their bosses anger. "And two, the magic of this island is real. He didn't survive because he was smart or because he was some secret badass, he survived because the light ensured so." He turns back to me turning down his voice. "Geez look at your skin, did you stab yourself with some glass? No don't tell me you ate some ya dumb fuck. That's amateur hour buddy." He laughs before stepping back and turns towards the hole before speaking again to the room.

"Thank you are all for being here today, helping us get here today. Today we take this island, take it from the feigning dynasty of bourgeoise that has reigned since our inception as a state. We will give the island to the people, with this river, we will stand to take the world."

"I thought this was about selling drugs, when'd you decide to become a revolutionist." I speak up but not before coughing up a significant amount of blood.

"Ah, he speaks. The drugs were merely to finance our dreams. They will continue to play a more role in our global schemes as with the river we shall enhance and diversify our stock beyond the realm of standard narcotics."

"The world will come after you."

"They will." He kneels in front of me, lowering his head so were on the same eye level so he can whisper, "And I will be ready." He stands, removing his jackets, shirt and shoes before again addressing the crowd, his arms extended outward.

"Today, who we were before dies. Who I was before now, dies. When I arise, all shall address me as Lord. Simple yes? Any who fall this will be terminated form our cause immediately. Agreed? Good." He turns towards one of his closer underlings and whispers a few words before again approaching the hole. As he prepares to dive, strength build in my legs as the guards once holding me down had since loosened their grip.

"No!" I scream, darting from the ground and catching him midair. The guards stumble in surprise as we both tumble into the hole, the rivers strong current ripping us away, through underground twists and bends. Before I black out, I remember the current slamming me against the jagged gemmed wall of the underground stream, still I hold onto Ceelos by an ankle, he was not going to get away from me no matter the circumstance

Legends say the talkative spirit disappeared when Harold the Second vanished, but something told me to stop him. Something told me to emerge from this victorious, something told me I'd be the last thing that mattered, the only thing that nattered. I heard Jennys' voice, along with my parents and grandparents. All in unison telling me to wake up and run.

I awake on a shore underground, black sand, the shining light river waving calmly as I sit up and examine the large set of caverns. I look out in the waters and I see Ceelos wading in the shallow, his hands lightly breezing the surface of the sparkling lake.

"This is why your girlfriend died. So, I could achieve godhood. I remember you now. Changing your name means nothing to what is now the infinite. For your remarkable effort, I shall bury you within the very walls of this great cavern. That is your only honor now. Solidius shall die, but first Ill warm up with you!" He extends at arm to me quick, flicking water from the river as his arm begins to shine brightly and from into an exoskeleton gauntlet of condenses light and energy. Blasts begins to burst from his palm towards me, instinct propels me into the air, flipping over his head as he continues blasting away against the walls and ceiling.

As I connect the surface of the water with my left hand I push myself back into the air, my righthand forms into an odd cannon with an accompanied scope made of light. Taking aim, I take a single shot that hits Ceelos off guard in his right shoulder. The bolt bursts through his back and he stumbles down, taking a knee in the now angry waving water.

I grip a stalactite above the river, preparing for a second shot, aiming at his head.

"Chuck!" I yell. "You shouldn't have killed Jenny! I would've left you alone and went on my mary fucking way" I take the next shot as he looks directly at me, the shot hits him in his left eye. As his lifeless body falls over into the river I whisper to myself before loosening my grip on the rock. "Then I wouldn't be here."

I let go completely and fall into the river a few yards from where his body floated about.

"I should be in Africa by now." I continue wading up the shore and onto the sand. "Well I guess I can just fly there myself now eh? That should be cool. How would I bring my luggage though? Forget it I'll just get new stuff when I'm there. Maybe those goons upstairs and loan me a few hundred bucks if they pooled in."

Instinct tells me to move to the left a few inches, blindly I follow as a bolt of lightning blasts past my head, exploding against the wall a few yards away. The explosion sends me backwards on my rear. I quickly manage to my feet and turn to see Ceelos standing in the river, his entire body now covered in an exoskeleton of both intense and condensed light now tinted purple. A light fog picked up throughout the cavern, the lightning of the waters began to spark a weird dark black and a haze of dark lilac seeped over everything.

"You want to go to Africa so bad. I'll send you to Africa. I'll send you to Africa in a cardboard box!" He charges me as a large blade forms in between in hands about nine feet long and about a foot wide. I leap over his head, his bulky armor already proving useless against my agility and freedom. Two blades form going down my arms from my hands and I begin slicing away chinks in his armor.

We begin a dance of energy and edge as we continued for some time. He was too big with his thick lightning armor, too angry as he continued to yell and road madly. He struggled to keep up with me as I continued my strategy of dodging and swiping and dodging and swiping.

"CLARK!!!" He yells, splitting his giant sword into two before throwing them both into the waters. They land as he expected them too, like darts in the lawn. He turns towards me again and like a rocket he charges with his fist both up high ready to slam down. I catch his hands and we lock for a moment before he breaks it and both our arms fall to our sides for a micro second. Up against the wall and needing to act now, I threw a few electrically charged jabs at his sides that he just flinched at. He smirked before coming with a surprise right hook, I duck just in time and he takes out a chunk of the wall.

"I should've killed you in Gallup! I'll smash your face into the ground until its nothing!" Again, he charges, I somersault between his lumbering legs at a moment's notice and begin stabbing him violently form behind with the again formed blades running down my arms. I extend the bladed tips to penetrate his armor and the flesh beneath and he roars from the quick jabs of agony. He turns swinging his arms wide, I dance between them. I fell as though he's operating on a different temporal wavelength. I am quicker, I can see further. But his strength is focused and yielding, his raw anger powers this madness, his lust for control and godhood has consumed him and rage beckons him far beyond the peaks of sanity. All is lost for this man's well-being, choices made long ago sculpted the monster before me, he is beyond redemption and death is his only penance, his only reward.

I crotch under another wild swing, electricity sizzling in my legs as I kick him backwards into the waters just beyond his two swords. I hadn't noticed before, but the swords were at the center of growing cyclones in the water, the same phenomenon followed Ceelos. The waters whipped madly around the three anomalies as to keep away from them.

"What is this?" He came to his knees in the river bed and examined the waters around him keep their distance. "Focus, focus, focus... enough games nameless, I have bigger fish to fry!" He proceeds forward towards the swords as the waters moved as he walked as to create a path. I could tell something was happening, the water was denying him. He was too enraged to see it now as he grabbed his twin broad swords, plucking them from the exposed soft mud.

"You're not worthy Chucky boy! The energy rejects you, it sees into your schemes and past!" I taunt him, still trying to formulate a plan, just attempting to stall him in, possible anger him to the point he makes a mistake I can take advantage of. "It can sense the darkness inside you I'm sure, you reek of dishonesty and selfishness." Ceelos begin to rush forward with the swords at the ready behind him.

"I'll cut you into pieces and fry you in oil over the raging flames of this accursed island!" Ceelos voice begins to darken and lower, twisting darkly. His swords had wrapped around his wrist and slithers up his arms. I could see his body working overtime, veins popping, glowing profusely. He was pushing too hard, easily I vault over him, sending him crashing into the wall. I recover quick from the somersault and aim a hand towards the dust cloud I knew he'd emerge from when I hear a whimper. Its him. Softly crying from either pain or something else I couldn't be sure. Uneasy I lower my hand and approach the dissipating cloud and the lightly crumbling hole in the wall he'd created.

"Why does this have to be so difficult?" I hear him say softly to himself almost whimpering, laying on the floor, seemingly drained of all energy.

"Dagger?" I reach a hand towards him to help him up when he bolts upright, and his eyes burst white as does his veins once again and he charges me, tackling me and we both tumble out of the small damaged area back onto the shore of the lightning lake. We begin exchanging blows back and forth, switching between him on top and me on top for several moments of struggling and horizontal dancing.

"Piece of shit!" He calls me a few times. "Son of a—" He says before I smash his face into the rocky pavement before he kicks me off of him. My lip bleeding, I rise slowly from the gravel as he does the same. Limply he gets into another fighting stance and waves me to come forward.

"You get more training than me over there or what? It doesn't matter. I've been building, you see. What have you built? Whatever it is I can tell you this, nothing else comes close to my shit." He charges with a backwards roundhouse, blocking it with my arm I quickly counter with a few jabs up his legs into his stomach. Sparks of white electricity fly with each block and hit, briefly illuminating the damp stillness of the cavern around us.

"Not long after you found your calling in some cave in New Mexico, the raids were finished. The cartels were finished in that hemisphere, I was transferred to The EC." He pulls back for a moment.

"The Entropy Committee huh? And I thought I was a sick dog." He replies before coming again full force, this time manifesting a small blade along his right for arm. He slices my side one good time before I manifest e set of twin blades of my own, running down both arms.

“How many murdered innocents overseas weigh on your conscience Allen Clark, what propels you to try and stop me? You’re not uniformed so what are you off duty of is this some sort of government funded excursion. You push much too hard, surely this cant be over your druggie friend back there.” He likes to talk, this time I charge, he tries to block a fury of swipes, but I land a few insufficient shots on his arms and legs. The wounds heal before my attacks are over, so I pull back to reevaluate, we were both overpowered, I had to think differently.

“Is this all for… god, what was that sluts name, Janessa, Jaresa, Joany?”

“Jenny you fuck, and yeah, this is strictly for her at this point. The Entropy Committee was gonna catch you eventually so maybe me doing their jobs for them will net me some points. See, I had a chance to get outta here before you dragged me down here. Now, I’ll be lucky if they give me a second after all the paperwork and debriefing they’ll subject me too once I bring them your head.”

“Enough with all of this Clark, I’ve got better things to attend to, I’d like to snap your spine quickly and end this immediately.”

“Try.” We both charge. I overpower him pushing him back into a wall unleashing a barrage a body and face blows that begin the crumble the wall behind him, the power literally shaking the foundations of the cavern. He kicks back into the opposite wall and zooms towards me, smashing me completely through the dark rocky wall into another small cavern devoid of light at all.

Our electrified bodies provided the only light as we continued exchanging blows in the dark. At one point, I heard the sound of his blade slicing through the silent still air so I countered with a small shield materialized up my arm just he hit. Through the attacks I grab him and toss him as I as I could into the wall and begin stomping until we are in yet another cavern, this one lit by a small blue florescent above a metal door opposite the long subterranean hall.

In my distraction he kicks me off him and grabs atop me beginning to throw a few jabs that I block easily.

"You're not even trying anymore Charlie." I kick him towards the light which I now realize is attached to an odd metal door painted to resemble the rest of the cave. He rises to his feet and notices the light and the fake wall before turning back to me as I charge him, slamming him up against the metallic part of the wall. He elbows me on the back as I begin kneeing him in the stomach up against the wall thudding loudly.

With all my strength I boost forward pinning up higher up the wall, he counters, twisting my momentum, spinning back around face first into the wall with a harder thud, grabbing me to the floor as the wall creaks. Slowly it falls inward revealing a dimly-lit warehouse filled to the ceiling with different crates and containers.

As I slowly come to my feet, he is already yards ahead of me into the warehouse examining a section of weapons and bombs, next to row of foggy glass containers. Each accompanied by a blinking computer panel that each read active. I could make out the silhouette of a strange creature within the containment glass.

"Ready to really put those powers to test?" Ceelos says wickedly just before smashing a handmade lightning axe into a metallic cylinder at the base of one of the upright containers. The impact sends smoke and shrapnel flying as an alarm begins to blare loudly throughout the dark facility. As the alarm volume shot up, the remaining crates begin to rumble and shake as the one he'd damaged catches fire and the glass slides down slowly.

As the smoke begins to clear, a monstrous black humanoid entity burst from the pod, grabbing with extended arms that reached a clear fifteen ten meters across the room. The being seemed to be coated in a thick carpet of a foul black sludge that dripped everywhere. It stepped out from the seven-foot pod standing at about ten full stretch. Its face was blank, covered by the same foul-smelling oil that dragged him down. Where he grabbed me, it began to burn and sting intensely, a burn far alike from the burn of fire, it felt like a chemical burn, salt in the wounds, acid in the eye type of burn.

As its poison physique battled with the lightning energy, slowing it ate away at my skin, slowing I was healed. There was no anesthetic, only adrenaline could distract me from the pain. I focus on Ceelos behind the tyrannical being he'd let loose, I focus hard as an energy field appears involuntarily around me keeping the monster from completely devouring me as I begin to close my eyes. Everything slows but me and I again focus on the laughter of the man on the other side of the room, blocking out the incestuous roar of the malformed creature restraining my arms. Through me closed eye lids I begin to see everything, I see beyond the now recognized subterranean storage facility, I see above the Theos Mountains, across the river Corinthian and beyond the shores of Theseus, above the Inggish hurricane wall and across the Pacific. I fly above, until the entire planet is in view at once, I see clouds circling above Sunlatveria. My home, the home I was set to abandon before today. Before I fall into any more thoughts of my own, I dive towards the clouding island in the distance.

Breaking through the clouds, I shoot for facility at what had to have been the speed of a blink. As I make contact the rock, I awake again in the warehouse room, on the verge of being overwhelmed by the unwieldly monstrosity. The maniacal Ceelos not even bother to run, just viewing from afar, laughing, taking revel in the death of a former comrade. My eyes shoot open, all I can see is the lightning energy building around me, I funnels my vision toward Ceelos and a burst of energy blast out of my chest shooting down the horrific beast in one shot.

I rise, detached from the floor I hover over the pile of smashed crates for a moment as Ceelos again begins to run, making his way through some sliding doors. My vision shows him locking it from the other side as he continues down a long hallway. Beyond that hall, I see a squadron of SEC security soldiers coming down three separate elevators with orders to purge and wipe the site. Their radios come in so clear, through the ether I hear everything and all around me and across the surface of the island.

I swear for a moment I connect with Solidius in his palace at Solitude but he blocks me, from him and his home. He must've sent the death squad, once he felt us in the caverns. As my mind wanders, I focus on Ceelos through the walls, his signature bright as he meets the hit squad full force. I watch from afar for a moment, hoping they'd kill him for me. But I know inside they'll fail. I spent years with the SEC, we knew nothing f the power of Solidius, the power of Sunlatveria. It only fueled our vehicles, our weapons, we didn't bother asking how the science worked. We were just hired killers and mercenaries after all.

He demolishes half their squad and as they begin a retreat I intervene, ignoring doors and halls, I move towards his signature with no delay, my own energy scorching so intensely it melts the steel and rock in so fast I move at a fixed pace. I break into the hall behind him as he raises his hand to kill a soldier left behind.

"Charles, no!" I yell, extending my hand, as I do a tentacle of condensed light and energy shoots towards him across thirty yards in about half a second. The arm wraps around his throat, I tug him towards me and he comes flying towards me. I ready a stance, as he gets into range I twist my legs and jump from the ground with a spinning roundhouse kick that sends him flying into the wall with a loud bang. I grab his neck from behind I restrain him against the wall.

"You served for this country and you dare strike down your brothers. These men signed the same contract as you, took the same oath as you!" Throughout the facility, the remaining SEC soldiers begin planting bombs, I hear as the individual detonators prime and begin a unified countdown.

"Fuck them!" Ceelos laughs again, face bloodied, his rage and conscience so misaligned that he can barely manage to break free from my hold, after a few failed struggles he gives in, accepting his fate.

"Kill me Allen, do it now or I will murder you and everyone else on this island of hypocrisy and bullshit!" Down the hall I hear the soldiers evacuating, a few stop in wonder of us before another tells them to move it. In my eavesdropping, Ceelos struggles again still pinned to the wall by me, both arms extending into large limbs of condensed white and blue.

"You shouldn't have killed Jenny. We wouldn't be here right now Charles!"

"She was bitch Clarke, a fucking whore of bitch, don't tell me you think she loved you? What a dumb cunt you are, that's why I didn't ask you to leave with me and the other guys back in New Mexico, too hung up on some chick half a world away to take pleasure in good old fashion murder." He uses his distracting tone to weaken my grasp, in that hesitation of a moment, he gets a second wind, bursting from my hold and spinning around in between my arms too long to catch him quickly enough as he punches me in the face a few times.

"Enough!" I yell, sending static discharge in every direction, I beam catches him by the shoulder and continues to blast him until he is down on one knee. All the rouge strands of electricity fade except the one shooting into him.

"You think this can hold me for long huh." He struggles to even say that he the thin beam of energy continues to shoot into him. I approach him slowly as the bring blue beam pirouetting across from me to him.

"You don't deserve this gift." I extend my open hand, a spark dances across my open palm. I clinch my fist killing it and Charles begin to wail harder in pain as the polarity of beam reverses and it turns a dark purple.

"You don't deserve life itself." I clinch my fist hard and lower my arm as the stream turns jet black. Charles again screams out in pains, convulsing as I sap away at his remaining lifeforce. The cries begin to cease and disappear until he is unresponsive, motionless, laying across the iron grated floor. Across the facility I hear all the bombs going off simultaneously, I look up towards the ceiling and close my eyes. I picture the airspace above the mountain range, my eyes burst open, tunneling on that scene, the clouds, the mountains rumbling, the incoming jets. I begin to rise from the floor and drill through the ceiling, through straight rock and dirt. My energy field melts and displaces all without much effort or harm to the surrounding bedrock.

I soon find myself above the Theos mountain range just floating about, detached to all, just hovering for a moment in the clouds. The mountain below me rumbling, crumbling from the inside, just as I predicted, jets incoming, three, no, six, coming from two separate air fields to investigate and provide air support for that SEC squad, I hope they got out alright. Through the mist and debris, I see the remains of that squad boarding helicopters just beyond what appears to be the facilities entrance.

Over the radios I hear the fighter pilots noticing me, the SEC squad vouching for me, saying not to fire, recounting what I'd did in the facility below. The jets break off but a few stay to circle the area a few times. All is calm for a moment and I contemplate what is next, do I still head to Africa or should I remain here. Before I can settle o a decision, I feel an approaching bullet or missile from the South and before I turn my head to see, I'm hit with what feels like a comet.

I fall like a ton of bricks, right through the thick jungle canopy on flat onto the forest floor. I jump back to my feet slowly, I could feel my power fading, that punch apparently knocked out a good portion of it I felt so significantly weaker. I look around, I sense nothing, I see nothing. My powers fail me as he appears from above, his cape fluttering in the wind softly, his armor, reflecting brightly the moons brightness into my eyes for a second.

"So, you're the one that killed that maniac Charles Dagger." He says, slowly listing towards the ground.

"Chancellor Solidius." Surprised I hesitate for a moment before answering. "Yes, and I apologize for getting your facility destroyed."

"Oh you saw what was in that storage area, it needed to be destroyed anyway."

"Y-you saw?!" I'd never seen him in person, but I recognized his young handsome face from the media.

"Of course, how do you think you won? You brought down an superpowered international criminal Allen, that's no easy feat, you have potential." He lands on the ground and walks right up to me, placing a hand on my chest. I feel an intense energy shoot throughout me, lightning running through my veins, energizing every atom. For an eternity I sit in this moment of immense power, then I realize.

"Wha-w-why?" I struggle to ask, with what I accept to be my last breath.

He doesn't respond. The energy overwhelms me and as if hit by a hundred overlapping orgasms, the light explodes, bursting from my chest, enveloping me into the light until my consciousness is all that remains for a few moments before even this is consumed.

Epilogue

Letters As I Go

Louise, my sister, please know that I love you more than bees and honey. We were rivals for so long under Edwins eye, we soon found we could not operate daily without one another. I'm leaving Sunlatveria, I'm leaving Earth actually. The spirits of the lake demand a great sacrifice of me. This is why father died sister, he refused his given mission, his purposed. No one else will succumb the same fate as I have accepted their almost impossible task. They pull me into the stars, a venture that will lead me to the other side of the cosmos and hopefully back.

I'm unsure how long I'll be gone, or if when I return you'll still be here. However, things turn out, please watch the kids from afar. I don't know what to tell them, so I told them nothing, tell them anything but the truth. I don't want that on my conscience, them knowing I abandoned them to chase down some dark evil a universe away like some cosmic detective. I know Alice would say 'you're just a man papa, your responsibilities lie here with your people, not up there.' Rex would be angry I'm not taking him. Its too dangerous, this force could consume the world that we know. The world we call home, it will come for us sooner or later.

Know this my beloved sister, as you prepare for your approaching nuptials, know that I will be there in spirit and thought. I will always love you and I will always have you in my mind, correcting my path as I go, straightening my ties, ensuring I'm standing upright. Do the same for the children. Rex is raw and has been resentful since both his mothers' deaths. Alice can handle herself, her mother taught her well. I wouldn't be surprised if she figured out a way to intercept me on my journey and bring me home. You must not let this happen, keep her there, keep her on Sunlatervia. I have a duty, a job that must be done. I will return home, rather it be in a few weeks or a few years.

Just hold it together for father sake please. Darkness and evil knock just beyond the threshold of reality, our light can repel them. Once I complete step one of my venture, our light will be able to destroy the intruding demons and seal them away for another eternity. I've learned, that we are not the first the fight this creature, nor are we the first to possess the light. The lake has opened doors for me sis, doors father refused to open. Why have you never taken it upon yourself to enlighten as we have? I am one with all light and energy. I see the rise of humanity along with its fall, I see the infinite loops of time that bind us to war and destruction over and over. I see a way to break that cycle and all that is necessary is a sacrifice on my part.

The future of the island is up to you, the children and the council. I can't think about it now. I've got to stay focused and motivated up here if I'm to complete y mission in hast. Thoughts of worry and regret infect my light, dimming my own power. I believe in you guys. Stay safe Louise, know ill always love you, you'll always have a place in my heart and you'll always be in my head.

Made in the USA
Lexington, KY
19 June 2018